Stay Feral!
Sage St
Cain ♡

Stay Feral!
Love it
Carol

the storms between us

GROVEWOOD INK
BOOK 1

SAGE ST. CLAIRE

Copyright © 2022 Sage St. Claire All rights reserved

The characters and events portrayed in this book are fictitious. Any similarity to real persons, living or dead, is coincidental and not intended by the author.

No part of this book may be reproduced in any form or by any electronic or mechanical means, including information storage and retrieval systems, without written permission from the author, except for the use of brief quotations in a book review.

This novel contains content intended for a mature audience only. Due to explicit language, graphic sex, detailed depictions of violence, and other possible triggers, reader discretion is advised.

ISBN-13: 9798218055271

Cover design by: Sage St. Claire

Printed in the United States of America

lets stay connected!

Scan here for Spotify playlist and Social Media for Sage St. Claire!

For My Husband
Thank you for proving to me that romance novels aren't always fiction. Your love is something I could never put into words. Here's to a lifetime together, babe. I love you.

playlist

Love Me More (Acoustic) - Sam Smith
All I Want - Lauren Spencer Smith
Black Mambo - Glass Animals
Falling - Harry Styles
Holy (Acoustic) - Chance the Rapper & Justin Bieber
Just You and I - Tom Walker
Train Wreck - James Arthur
White Flag - Bishop Briggs
First Date - Taylor Acorn
Easy - James TW
Let's Go Home Together - Ella Henderson & Tom Grennan
The Bones (Acoustic) - Maren Morris
September - James Arthur
I love you more - Avery Anna

Grovewood Ink Book 1

Artist Credit: James Dupper of Iron Rite Tattoos

prologue
EMBER

TWIN TELEPATHY. So many people think it's the real deal. Me? I have my doubts. If it were real, surely Everett could feel the pain and desperation I was feeling right now. I knew we wouldn't be together forever because that's obviously insane and a little gross for a brother and sister. But he must feel the fear and uncertainty coming off of me in waves. I felt the bottom fall out before he even said the words "I'm enlisting". I've always known he felt a pull to serve our country, but nothing could have prepared me for this day. We were both so desperate to leave our home behind and blaze our own trails. The feeling of not knowing where he will be or if he's safe overpowers any excitement I feel knowing I know a new adventure is awaiting me at Duke. "I'll see you soon, Sparky," are the last words I hear from him as he boards the bus and drives into the unknown. All of a sudden, I'm utterly alone. For the first time in my life, I'm starting my own journey.

one

4 YEARS LATER

Ember

MUSIC IS BLARING through the thin walls of my shitty apartment. I'm glad I only have a week left before I leave this place, diploma in hand. When I told my parents I wanted to study English Lit, their eye rolls spoke volumes. Making a career out of reading or writing seemed like a joke to two Yale Business School grads, but I knew it called to me. Even the fact that I got into Duke wasn't enough to please them. But being on the front lines of the literary world excites and fulfills me in a way nothing else ever has. I honestly can't wait to dive in.

The past four years here haven't been easy. I've had to learn how to function as my own person, no longer one half of a pair. Here, I'm just Ember. I'm not not the other Blake twin. Being separated from Everett has been the most difficult part. Seeing him through video calls eases my anxieties, but it's not the same as seeing him face to face. Growing up with parents who were completely unconcerned about the children they were supposed to raise caused us to be self-reliant at a young age. If he needed someone to cheer him on at a lacrosse game, he looked for me in the stands. When people made fun of me for constantly having my nose in a book, Everett stood up for me. We protected each other. We raised each other. I was terrified of being alone after he left for the Marines. I couldn't imagine taking on such an important life event like college without him by my side. It's been a challenge to discover who I am and who I want to be. Somewhere in the halls of this university, I found the woman I am today. She's strong-willed and confident but still quiet, like the eye of a storm. After 4 years, I feel like a different person. I still love to share my accomplishments and troubles with Ev, but I've become comfortable in my skin. I know I've accomplished great things here at Duke and I'm proud of the person I am.

Severing my ties with my ex, Justin, was the last piece I needed to truly get myself together. I met Justin during my second year here. I was reading over an essay in the courtyard outside the campus cafe and he played the old "trip over the girl while playing football" trick. Unfortunately, I fell for it. You would think a woman as well-versed in the greatest love stories ever written would be more aware of what bullshit hides behind a trick like that, but he was a smooth talker. He always told me how beautiful he thought I was and how he couldn't live without me. At the time, I thought it was endearing. But it wasn't long before I realized the monster that hid behind his fake façade. Looking back now, I'm disappointed in myself for allowing him to worm his way into my heart and my head.

He had his moments when he would make snide comments about my behavior or appearance, but he would always brush it off as a joke and ease my worries. The first time I felt genuine fear with him was during a group outing with all our friends. We were dating for almost a year by then and things seemed okay, but it was just an illusion. We went to a local club and were all drinking, dancing, and having a great time. His friend Connor made a sexy librarian joke about my glasses and put his arm around me, giving me a punch on the arm. Justin lost his mind, shoving Connor off of me and accusing me of coming on to him. Later that night, once we got back to my apartment, he called me a whore and told me I needed to be more careful not to embarrass him. Fire flared in his eyes as he grabbed me by my elbows and screamed at me, telling me never to behave that way again.

The next morning, I saw the dark bruises on my skin and knew I wouldn't put myself in that position again. I asked my best friend, Kelsea, to come over with the football player she was dating to help me pack Justin's shit. I sent him a text telling him I never wanted to see him again. We changed the locks on my apartment that day, dropped his boxes off outside his place, and I felt confident that would be the end.

Unfortunately, I was very wrong. I started receiving notes on my door and car, flowers delivered to the desk in my apartment building, and countless calls and texts at all hours begging me to take him back. He swore he was drunk that night and would never have acted that way otherwise. But I've never been a weak person when it comes to speaking my mind and standing my ground. I changed my number and told all of my professors and campus security about the situation. They assured me they would counsel him and he wouldn't bother me any more. Two years later, and I've seen him around campus a handful of times. Sometimes he's there when I walk out of the cafe or the library, but it's not a big campus. Unfortunately, I'm bound to run into him whether I like it or not. He's tried talking to me, apologizing or telling me he'd like to hang out, but I'm not interested.

Graduation is a week away, now. I'm only focused on moving out of here and starting my internship in South Carolina, where I can be closer to my brother. After he finished his tour in the Marines, he settled down in a coastal town about ten miles from Charleston and opened a tattoo shop with some buddies from his unit. He invited me to stay with him after graduation and I jumped at the chance. I was offered a paid internship with an independent publishing group and given the opportunity to work remotely, allowing me to travel anywhere I please. To say it was a total dream is an understatement. I've never felt tethered to a single person in my life, but more to places. I was stuck in west Texas because of my parents, stuck in North Carolina because of Duke, and now I would be tethered to South Carolina to start over somewhere new. This time, I wouldn't mind. Being twins, Everett and I always had a propensity to fall into place together. We hung in the same friend circles in school, seldom separate from each other the entire time we were growing up. When he suggested I come stay with him in his three-bedroom townhouse, it was a simple decision.

I close my laptop and textbook after submitting the last of my final essays and breathe a sigh of relief. After four years, the constant all-nighters and piles of Red Bull cans have finally felt worth it. The realization that I did this solely for myself brings a watery smile to my face. I wouldn't say I'm an overly emotional person, but I am proud of myself for not backing down when my parents told me this degree would be a waste.

A knock on my door shakes me from my thoughts, and I reluctantly shuffle to answer. Hopefully, it isn't anyone important because my comfy grey sweats and Green Day t-shirt aren't the most glamorous. When I look through the peephole, I see a woman standing there holding a long white box in her hands. I open the door and remove the chain hesitantly.

"Are you Ember Blake?" She asks, looking impatient with one hand propped on her hip and the other clutching the box.

"I might be. Who's asking?" I fire back, irritated by her attitude.

"Look, it's been a long day already and I have a ton of deliveries left. Can you just sign here?" She shoves a clipboard towards me with a delivery log attached.

"Who is this from? I'm not expecting any deliveries." I ask her, but she rolls her eyes and snatches the clipboard from my hands with a huff.

"Couldn't tell ya, I just deliver the boxes. Maybe there's a card inside." She pushes the box into my hands and turns, walking down the stairs without another word.

I take the box into my apartment, setting it down on the kitchen counter. The long rectangle is an odd shape compared to the dozens of packages of books I'm used to receiving. I slide the lid off to reveal a dozen long-stemmed roses with a card and picture stacked on top. I crinkle my nose at the powerful aroma pouring out of the box. Ugh, roses. My absolute least favorite flower. They remind me of funerals and I've never been a big flower lover, anyway. Lifting the card out of the box, my hands begin to shake a bit. I immediately recognize my name written in Justin's heavy, aggressive script across the envelope. I take a steadying breath and open the card.

"Ember,

Congratulations on your upcoming graduation, my love. I'm so proud of you for achieving this accomplishment. Knowing there's nothing standing in the way of us being together makes me so happy. You can give me and this relationship the attention I deserve now. I've waited two years to bring you back where you belong and the wait is finally over. I'll be seeing you soon.

Justin"

An icy shiver runs down my spine as I drop the card and finally see the photo laying on top of the flowers. It's a picture of me in the campus coffee shop with my head thrown back, laughing at something Kelsea said. I vaguely remember her telling me some joke about the fraternity bathroom she had to use last week. I know I didn't see Justin in the cafe that day. Has he been watching me? Photographing me without me knowing?

I fall into the chair at my bar with my head in my hands. How did I end up with this psycho? I knew he could be aggressive, but this feels different. Years of watching true crime documentaries tell me this is borderline crazy stalker behavior. This is definitely not something I saw coming. My hands shake as I reach for my phone. I dial the number that brings me peace in any storm.

Everett answers on the second ring, "Hey Emby, what's up?" His voice is an instant balm to the fear burning through my veins. I take a deep breath before answering him to mask my unease.

"Hey Ev, just checking in. I just submitted my last assignment and I'm all packed and ready to head your way."

"I can't wait, Sparky." I hear the smile in his voice already. "Are you sure you need to wait another week?"

Sighing, I brace myself for this conversation, not wanting to raise any concern in him, "That's actually why I'm calling," I try to force some false excitement into my voice, "I don't really feel like waiting around here for no reason. Mom and Dad already said they aren't coming to graduation and honestly, I couldn't care less about walking across the stage just to get my diploma. I'm thinking about just picking it up tomorrow and heading your way this weekend. I know it's earlier than we planned, but what do you think?"

I hear the buzz of a tattoo gun in the background and know that he must be working. "That sounds great, Emb. I'm ready whenever you are, no point in waiting if you don't want to. You're welcome to head down here whenever you want."

Relief floods through my body, knowing I'll soon be putting distance between Justin and I and starting my life somewhere new. I don't say anything to Everett about the box or the situation with Justin. Keeping something from him makes my stomach churn. I've never kept secrets from my brother, but he was always wary of Justin. He said he gave him a bad feeling, and he didn't think Justin deserved me. Turns out he was 100% right. I can't imagine what he would say about this recent development.

"Ok Ev, I'm gonna get things settled here tomorrow and I'll be in Grovewood by Sunday. Sound good?"

"Perfect, Sparky. My client just got here, so I gotta run. Let me know if you change your mind about needing help. I can be there tomorrow," he says. Hearing him use my childhood nickname brings a smile to my face and releases some of the tension I've been holding onto.

"No, it's okay. I can handle it. I'll see you Sunday!" I force some cheeriness into my voice and quickly hang up before he catches on.

two

Elijah

THE SHRILL TONE of my alarm jolts me out of my latest nightmare. I've tried for years to rid myself of the images of everything I've seen and done over my time in the Corp, but it's no use. Those memories are burned into my soul, hardening my heart a little more each time I relive them. The faint sound of gunfire still rings in my ears as I sit up in bed. Rubbing my hands over my face to clear my head, I take a deep breath and brace my elbows on my knees. After my second trip overseas, I finally agreed to see a therapist. Funny thing about therapy is that they always want you to talk about the one thing you're trying to avoid most. I tried my best not to take my anger and impatience with the situation out on the therapist, but I don't think I succeeded. The handful of anti-depressants and anti-anxiety meds I take daily are a testament to my success in the mental health department.

I throw my legs over the side of the bed and walk to the bathroom. I turn on the shower faucet as hot as it goes and watch as it quickly fills the bathroom with steam. The memories haunting me are the reason I'm happy living my life alone, one day at a time. I work, I ride, sometimes I blow off a little steam with a mindless fuck, but I never get attached. It's not worth it. I'm not worth it. It's not self-pity or any of that other bullshit. It just is what it is. I check my phone and see that it's just now noon. I've got about 4 hours before my first client shows up at the shop. That should give me enough time to swing by the plantation house and check on things before I have to go in.

I take a quick shower, doing my best to scrub away the memory of last night's dreams, and I'm ready to go in record time. I come downstairs and hear silence in the kitchen and living room. Everett must still be asleep. I'm pretty sure he mentioned something about having a client around 1:30 today, and that's in about twenty minutes. I pound on his door and wait quietly for a response. A miserable sounding groan filters through the door and I chuckle. He's obviously hungover.

"Dude, get up," I shout.

"Fuck off," he yells back, loud but muffled, so I'm sure he hasn't moved from his bed.

"You're gonna be late as hell if you don't leave right

now," I grab my shit and walk towards the door. Cuss words fly and something hits the ground with a thud, which just makes me laugh even harder. He may be a dipshit, but he's my favorite one. I climb on my bike and point it towards the gas station. I guess I'll fuel up before heading over to the plantation to see how far along we've progressed on all my latest projects.

I bought the plantation house about a year after me and Ev moved to Grovewood. I needed a project to keep myself busy and I've always loved being able to work with my hands. Since then, I've been able to bring my visions to life in a way I never knew I wanted to. I take pride in that house like nothing else I ever have before. I've literally built it with my bare hands and that feels damn good.

As I make my way through the streets of our sleepy town, I take a minute to appreciate the life I've built here. It may not look like much, but to me it's everything. When I was younger, I always assumed I'd end up just like my piece of shit father. By now he's probably in jail or dead, but I wouldn't know. I've tried my best over the past decade to make sure I don't become him. I don't run from my problems the way he did.

I pull my bike to a stop at the gas station on the edge of town. I wish our town would invest in some newer pumps, so I didn't have to go inside to pay, but I can't avoid Candace forever. She's a sweet girl, killer body, and always down for anything, anytime. Lately though,

I've been hearing that hint of wanting more every time we talk. I'm always transparent anytime I hook up with a chick. I'm not interested in being anybody's boyfriend, just looking for a good time.

I walk straight to the counter and lay down a twenty and a bottle of water. "Can I get $20 on pump 3, please?" I watch as she leans over the counter, pushing her tits together like it isn't obvious.

"Hey Eli, been a few weeks since I've seen you. How've you been?" She runs her fingers through her bleach blonde hair, attempting to be sexy. Sometimes I wonder what my dick is thinking every time I dial her number.

"Yeah, I'm good, Candy. Can I get the gas? I've got shit to do." I'm really not trying to be a dick. I just don't have time for this. Last time we hooked up, she begged me to stay the night with her. I got out of that place like my ass was on fire. I don't sleep next to anyone. Not anymore. And even if I did, it definitely wouldn't be her. The whiny tone of her voice is especially irritating me today, and I'm doing my best to hold on to the little patience I have left. She brushes her fingers across my hand as she reaches for the cash. I can tell she's trying as hard as she can to be seductive. It's just not working for her.

"Of course," she says with a wink, "you can have anything you want, baby."

Baby. Absolutely fucking not. I've never been a fan of

pet names and I'm sure as fuck not gonna become one now. "Thanks." I try to be as cold as possible, not wanting to lead her further into her delusion that there's something more between us than a quick fuck.

"I get off at 8 tonight if you want to come by," she bats her fake eyelashes hard enough to kick up a stiff wind and I can't take this shit anymore.

"I'll pass, thanks. Bye, Candace," I turn and walk out without another word. I know she's giving me a go to hell look behind the counter, but I don't give a shit. Hopefully, she gets the hint and doesn't call me anymore at all. I'm really not an asshole, but I've made it crystal clear to her I'm not interested in a relationship. Still, she pushes me every time.

I drop my ass onto the seat of my bike and start the engine. The deep rumble of the pipes is enough to give me a hard on every time. I'm not one of those guys who are obsessed with their cars, but I can appreciate a sexy machine. I pull out onto the main road and make my way towards the plantation.

three

Ember

"ARE you sure you don't wanna walk in the graduation ceremony?" Kelsea asks for the thousandth time today. I turn around, pushing the last of my bags into the back of my Jeep and slamming the door hard.

"Yes, Kels, I'm 100% sure that I don't give a single shit about walking across the stage with only you in the audience to clap for me," I rolling my eyes at her insistence.

"That's so not true! Jake will totally be there to clap for you, too!" She motions behind us to her boyfriend, leaning lazily on the hood of her Subaru. I'm sure this is the last place he wants to be on a Saturday night, but he hasn't complained.

I've appreciated having both of them here to carry my minimal amount of belongings down from my third floor apartment and into the small trailer hooked up behind Charlie, my faithful Jeep. You never really know how much stuff you have until you have to move it. I see Kelsea shrug uncomfortably, and I move to pull her in for a hug. She's been my lifeline for three years here, and I don't know how I would have made it through without her.

I think back to when I met Kelsea during my sophomore year at Duke. She was a freshman rushing Kappa Phi Nu. A pledge prank gone wrong left her in the library in nothing but her bikini on a Monday night in December.

"Those stupid BITCHES!" I heard someone screech from the reference section. As she strutted down the line of study desks looking like Malibu Barbie, she stopped in front of me. "Excuse me, I know you're studying, but can I borrow this?" She asked, motioning to my sweatshirt laying on the table. I looked up at her, slightly stunned by the sight of this girl in her hot pink bikini and heels in such a somber setting.

"Um... sure. I mean, obviously yes, of course." I tripped over my words as she swiped it off the desk and pulled it over her raven hair.

"Thanks so much. My 'friends' thought it would be just hilarious to run off with my clothes in the middle of a snowstorm. That's what I get for thinking Kappa would be a 'joyful experience' like my mom described. Do you know if the campus transport service picks up this late?" She asked as she tapped away on her hot pink iPhone. Something told me she's had a thing for pink.

"Um, I'm not sure. My apartment is right next door, so I've never had to use it." I looked around and realized it was well past midnight and I was the only one left in the library. How did that always happen to me?

"Well, shit. I guess I'll have to call an Uber or something. Only creeps are out this late. Damnit! I'm such a fucking idiot sometimes." She seemed to be talking to herself more than to me. The introvert in me wanted to tell her I hoped she found a way home and leave it at that, but I remembered how scared I was during my freshman year before I got my bearings around campus.

"My apartment is right next door and we look about the same size. Do you wanna come over and at least put on a few more layers before you try to trek across campus?" I wasn't sure if I wanted her to say yes or no. She looked at me like I'd grown three heads, and I instantly wondered if I'd said the wrong thing.

"Are you for real?" She asked, barely above a whisper. "I don't think anybody has offered something so nice in the three months since I came here. Are you sure? I mean, I could be an axe murderer? I'm not. Definitely not. But I could be." I laughed at her candid nature and she seemed to relax a bit.

"I'm sure I couldn't leave you stranded here and still

sleep tonight, so yeah, I'm sure." I told her as I packed up my books and threw my backpack over my shoulder.

We hurriedly made the short walk across the parking lot to my apartment building, dodging ice patches as we went. It amazed me how quickly she moved in those 4-inch heels without falling on her ass, something I could never master. We made the climb up to the third floor and hurried into my apartment. I could see her shivering even though she tried to mask it.

"Do you want some tea or coffee or something? I'm sure you're freezing over there," I asked, yelling at her from down the hallway as I walked towards my room. I grabbed my thickest yoga pants and my soft Blue Devils t-shirt and brought them back to the kitchen.

"Yeah, coffee sounds amazing right now," she said, pulling the cozy clothes on over her bikini and dropping her heels on the floor by the door.

The next hour was filled with sharing our favorite bands and books over coffee and the toasted pop tarts I had in my cabinet. I told her she could crash on the couch and call campus transportation in the morning to be safe. The next day, and every day after, Kelsea and I became the constant in each other's lives.

Pulling myself into the present, I see her eyes shining with unshed tears and I squeeze her tighter. "I'll only be four hours away, Kels. You can come visit whenever you want to and text or call me any time you need me," I tell her, trying to be reassuring but holding back my own tears. "I know, but it won't be the same as seeing your face every day. I'll manage, I'm sure. Jake will just have to take your place in our Friday night rom-com marathons." She jokes as Jake rolls his eyes behind her. She gives my hand one last squeeze, telling me to drive safely and call her as soon as I get to Everett's place.

I climb into the driver's seat and glance at her in the rear-view mirror. I could have waited one more night to make the trip, but I can't stand the thought that Justin could be watching me right now. I have to get out of here and I prefer driving at night, anyway. It's quiet and there's not as much traffic on the roads. I can be alone with my thoughts and decide how to deal with the Justin situation.

As I drive past the Durham city limit sign, I feel the tension slowly begin to drain from my body. This is the right choice. I just know it.

four

elijah

THE KNUCKLES on my left hand ache as they wrap around my tattoo gun. I've been working on this piece for over three hours now and it's looking sweet as fuck. When this chick came sauntering in with her fuck-me red heels and black leather shorts, I thought for sure I was going to be turning away some drunk party bitch, but she actually had a plan and a great idea. She told me the story of how her grandpa passed last week and she wanted to do something to remember him. She brought me a design that she'd drawn herself, which I rarely do, but the dagger and wildflower combo was a beautiful piece.

Surprisingly, she's been pretty chill about it, too. I wouldn't recommend the spine for anybody's first tattoo, but she was adamant, and I wasn't in the mood to argue. I ease up, setting my rig down and stretching my hand out wide. Wiping away the extra blood and ink, the vivid red color pops against her pale skin.

"Need a break?" I ask her, standing and stretching my back and arms.

I see her wipe a single tear from the corner of her eye and nod. "Yeah, I'll grab a smoke and a snack and be ready to start again in about 10 minutes. Sound good?" She asks, trying and failing to mask the sadness in her voice.

"Perfect. Meet you back here in 10." I grumble, making my way to the small kitchen we built onto the back of our shop.

If you told me ten years ago that I would be a partner in my own business by 29, I would have laughed in your face. But I was a completely different man then. That man was a punk ass 19-year-old with a chip on his shoulder and a tendency to have run-ins with the law. My last offense was the same as all the rest. The Barney Fife-like sheriff in my hometown back in Louisiana caught me tagging an abandoned train car for the fourth time and decided he'd had enough of my bullshit. The judge gave me two options, spend a year in county for being a repeat offender or enlist to "straighten myself out". Even though the draft hadn't been a thing for the last fifty years, backwoods towns like mine operated on a different level. No way was my ass spending a second in jail, so I chose the latter. Sheriff Bates followed me all the way to the enlistment center in Baton Rouge the next day.

The day I left for basic training, my ma and sister were there to wave me off from the bus stop. I felt a pang of guilt slash through me, knowing I was responsible for taking care of them. So far, I was doing a shitty job at it.

My dad skipped town the day my sister turned 5 and left my mom with an empty savings account and two months of overdue bills. She tried her best to work doubles as an ER nurse to support us, but I knew it broke her down. I took odd jobs fixing motorcycles and cars around town to help out. I always had a knack for making things run, even though my heart was never really in it. But money was money, and we needed it. I spent my nights sketching and sneaking out to tag random overpasses and buildings around town. I had an itch to see my art on display and it couldn't be contained.

My ma's arms squeezed tight around my neck and I wrapped my arms around her, feeling the slight shaking of her shoulders as she cried. I knew this wasn't what she wanted for me, but it beat the alternative. "It's gonna be okay, Ma. You'll see me again before you know it and I'll be able to send way more money home to help you and Aurora." I told her, stuffing my emotions back down my throat.

"I don't care about the money, Elijah Jude. I just want you to be safe. Just promise me you'll be safe." She pleaded, her blue-grey eyes swirled with the flood of emotion she was trying to hold back.

"I promise I'll do my best, Mom. Just take care of this brat for me." I joked, punching my little sister lightly in the shoulder. At 9 years old, she was wise beyond her years out of necessity, and I hated that for her.

"Ha-ha, so funny. Now get lost, loser," she threw back at me as she snaked her arms around my waist and squeezed me tight.

"I'll miss you most, Bug. Take care of Mama." I whispered to her as I kissed the top of her head. I boarded the bus and watch them wave as I marched forward into my new life.

A knock on the doorway drags me from my memories and I turn to see my business partner and best friend, Everett, standing in the doorway. We opened this shop together last year after we both decided not to re-enlist for another tour. When he told me of his idea to open a tattoo shop near Charleston, I immediately knew I wanted in on the action.

"Hey, that fine piece of ass you've been working on is back in your chair and waiting for you. Please tell me you're going to break your client rule for that one because DAMN." He stresses, peering around the corner to take a second look at her. At 22 years old, he's the true definition of an unapologetic man-whore, but I wouldn't have him any other way.

I chuckle at his crass description of the girl and

brush past him. "Never gonna happen, bro. That's all you," I say, heading back to my station.

"Hey, I just wanted to remind you that my sister will be in tonight. She said she left Durham around 7, so she probably won't come through 'til about midnight. I'm supposed to have a client at 10:30, so I told her to just swing by here to get the keys," he says, hanging halfway into my station, eyeing the buxom blonde laying on my table.

"Yeah, I remember. I can't imagine a female version of your ugly ass, so hopefully she got the good genes." I joke, snapping my black gloves back over my hands and getting my tattoo gun ready for round two. "I'll make sure I keep an eye on the door and send any stray women your way, bro." I hear him laughing loudly as he retreats to his side of the studio and I get back to the work at hand.

five

Ember

ROLLING through the small coastal town of Grovewood is like taking a step back in time. As I pass through rows and rows of hundred-year-old trees dripping in Spanish moss, I can't help but feel at peace. Something about this place makes me feel like I belong here, which is a foreign feeling for me. Never in my 22 years have I felt truly at home anywhere. Looking around the main square, I can see myself editing a manuscript at the little coffee shop on the corner. The beautiful park across the street would be a great place to read on a breezy spring day. I could really make a life here.

Checking my GPS again to make sure I'm heading in the right direction, I see a text from my brother telling me he's going to be stuck at the shop late with a client. Fine by me. I'll enjoy having some quiet time to myself to snoop around his place and make myself at home. He tells me to stop by to grab the keys, so I make a right down the side street up ahead and pull my Jeep to a stop in front of the neon sign that says "TATTOOS".

After four and a half hours of driving, I unfold myself from the driver's seat and stretch my aching muscles. For midnight on a Saturday in a small town, the shop seems to be pretty busy. I can see several people sitting on a couch in the lobby through the front window and it brings a smile to my face. I'm proud of what Everett has built here. Our parents were never the type to fawn over our accomplishments, so we always cheered for each other. Knowing my brother is carving out his own path here makes me absolutely thrilled for him.

I lock my Jeep and make my way through the front doors. The bell over the door signals my arrival, and I see a few patrons look my way before focusing back on their phones. The buzz of tattoo guns isn't a familiar sound for me and it puts me a little on edge. Nothing against tattoos or the people who have them, of course. I just can't imagine anything I would ever love enough to put on my body permanently.

"Hello?" I call out when nobody comes to the desk. I can see the clear divide down the center of the shop with two stations set up on each side. I remember Everett telling me something about having a partner from the Marines who also does tattoos and a few others who handle the business side of things.

"Just a sec, have a seat and somebody will be with you in a minute," a gruff voice shouts back at me.

"Um, okay. Do you have a bathroom? I've been driving for a while and I could really use it." I yell back, fidgeting uncomfortably.

"Jesus Christ, gimme a sec," I hear the voice mumble, sounding annoyed. I prop my hip against the desk, stare down at my scuffed vans, and wait for some acknowledgment.

"Something I can help you with?" I hear the deep timbre ask from right next to me, causing the air around me to electrify. I sweep my gaze up quickly from the floor and lock on to the most beautiful crystal blue eyes I've ever seen. Stunned by the power in his gaze, I stand silently, unmoving. We stare intently at each other for what feels like several long minutes. In reality, it was probably only a few seconds in time. The swirls of grey in his irises are too beautiful to look away from. It's as if I could reach out and touch the ocean behind his eyes.

Speak Ember. Words. Remember those? What is wrong with me? I internally chastise myself for my sudden loss of wits and physically shake my head to ease the tension surrounding us. My body heats with embarrassment and I clear my throat, hoping to expel the momentary insanity that seems to have overtaken me.

"Um, hi, sorry I'm just here for Everett," the words fall out in a rush like a clumsy teen with her first crush.

What is wrong with me? It's like I've never seen an attractive man in my life before! It's not like he's that good looking, right? HA! Who am I kidding? This is the most beautiful man I've ever seen. The slight tick in his jawline draws my eyes back to his face. And damn, what a face it is. A short, neatly trimmed beard lines his chin and jawline, and his deep chocolate brown hair is pulled back out of his face into one of those man buns hipsters usually sport. But there's nothing "hipster" about this man. He exudes strength and confidence with just one look.

My eyes quickly divert from his intense stare and take notice of the intricate designs trailing all the way from his knuckles, up his arms, and under his shirt sleeves. Instantly, I want to push his shirt up and out of the way so I can follow the path of ink marking his skin. Where that thought came from, I have no clue. I can't remember the last time I had a remotely sexual thought about a man. Sure, the guys at Duke were okay. But after Justin, I just kept my head down and focused on the diploma at the end of the tunnel. I didn't want to waste my time on a guy who just wanted a quick lay. Something tells me this man would keep any woman coming back for more.

I look up to realize he's just standing here staring at me, not saying a word. Did I say something stupid? I don't think so. But apparently I've lost all ability to think around this man, so who knows.

"Everett's with a client for the rest of the night. We don't have time for walk-ins tonight," the man snaps. He turns to walk back to his station and I feel the loss of his presence instantly.

"Wait! I'm Ember. I'm supposed to be meeting him here." I hope my brother at least gave someone the heads up I was coming tonight. "I'm supposed to be picking up the spare key to his place."

"*You're* Ember?" The man says, turning to look deeper at me and I suddenly feel very exposed. I've never been the type of girl who felt like I needed to dress nicely or wear makeup to impress a man. If you don't like me the way I am, then I don't have time for you. But standing here under the inquisitive gaze of this stranger, I wish I was wearing something nicer than my torn denim cutoffs and a Ramones t-shirt.

"Yeah. That's me. Ember Blake. Everett's sister. Not sure why I added that. Is he here?" I babble, wondering where my common sense has gone.

The man turns and walks further back into the shop without another word. He takes a right into the section opposite from his and I can hear him say something to whoever is back there.

"No shit? Sparky's here?!?" I hear the familiar resonance of my brother's voice from inside the room and then see his head peek out of the doorway. I give him a small wave and his smile stretches from ear to ear. "Emby! You made it! Give me a sec to get this wrapped up and I'll be right out." He yells, motioning to the client I assume is laying on his table. He turns to the mystery man with a nod. "Thanks Eli, this is the infamous Ember, by the way," he says, signaling in my direction. I can feel the heat from Eli's gaze on my face without meeting his eyes. Never have I felt such intense scrutiny in my life, and I shift uncomfortably.

I raise my hand in greeting towards Eli and he gives me a gruff head nod in return. "Elijah Harding. Heard a lot about you," he states very matter-of-factly and walks into his station, and out of my sight. I'm suddenly curious about what my brother has told him and why I care so much.

After using the bathroom, I take a seat in the waiting room. I finally take a second to look around the room at all the artwork covering the walls. They're covered from floor to ceiling in intricate, hand-drawn designs. Everything from delicate floral arrangements to skulls with flames and anything in between can be found here. I assume this is a collection of several unique artists to give customers ideas when they come in. Everett has always been the artistic one of the two of us, the right-brain to my left. But even with an analytical mind, I still love to fall into a good fiction novel. Mostly the "smut" as my mother calls it, but hey a girl has to get her rocks off somewhere.

My mind wanders back to Elijah and those beautiful ocean eyes. Now there's a man who would make an excellent book cover. I let my imagination fill in the blanks of what could be under his tight black t-shirt. Judging by the forest scene that wraps all the way around one arm, the tips of the trees disappearing under his sleeve, I don't think there's an inch of bare skin left under there. Shirtless Elijah? There's a view to make your mouth water. His jeans hung low on his hips, letting the slightest peek of his v-cut abs show through his shirt. The idea of running my fingertips down those abs sends a bolt of heat straight to my core. I push those thoughts from my head as I pull my phone out to shoot Kelsea a quick message to let her know I'm here.

six

Elijah

HOLY. F̲ucking. S̲hit.

That is the most beautiful woman I've ever laid eyes on. How have I not seen her in pictures before? I've lived and worked side by side with Everett for the last four years. Surely he's shown me a picture of them together, right? But I know there's no way I've seen her before. I would never forget those rich green eyes. The way they burned my skin as she scanned over my face and arms, inspecting every inch of my tattoos like she was entranced by them. No one has ever looked at me that way.

I know I've never had a problem with women. Before he was a piece of shit, my dad was actually a pretty good-looking guy and I take after him the most. At 6' 4", women see me coming from a long way off and have no problem embarrassing themselves to try impressing me.

But I have no interest in women like that. I could find a piece of ass anywhere. I'm just not enticed by blatant and fake flattery.

Ember doesn't strike me as the overtly sexual type. She's a stunner, albeit a short one, with a slim build but curvy in all the right places. The way she tripped over her words after I caught her checking me out tells me she's not usually so obvious in her attraction. But damn, that smile. Pure fucking sunshine. Even if it was an uncomfortable one, it stirred something in my chest that felt totally foreign to me. All I want now is to see that smile over and over again.

No. I have to stop this train of thoughts before it gets derailed. She's Everett's sister. He already explained to me that her last relationship was with some frat dickhead who basically made her swear off men for most of her college life. She's here to get on her feet and I won't interfere with that.

Wiping the extra blood and ink off of my client's back, I stand back to look at the work I've done. This is badass and she handled it like a champ.

"Mind if I take a picture for the wall?" I ask her.

"Go right ahead. You can take an extra one to remember me by if you want to," she purrs in her most seductive voice. Yeah, not gonna happen.

"Sorry, sweetness, I don't mess around with clients. But keep me in mind if you decide you need more work done. I'd be happy to oblige." I let her down easy and watch her face fall as I do. It's always been a rule of mine not to mix business with pleasure. You don't fuck where you eat and I'm not about to start now.

I walk her to the front desk to cash out and hand her a card with aftercare instructions. "Let me know if you have any problems with healing. Hopefully, you've got somebody who can help you out with keeping it clean."

"Well, you're welcome to help me out anytime." She says, placing her hand on my arm and batting her eyelashes like I'm really gonna fall for that shit. This chick is laying it on thick.

My eyes immediately dart to Ember sitting on the couch behind her and I see she's watching this encounter intently over the top of her phone. She looks almost irritated by the woman's forward approach, which brings a smirk to my lips.

"No thanks, have a good night." I tell the woman as I pull my arm out of her reach.

She shrugs, picking up her bag, and walks out the door. I watch Ember's eyes follow her through the window until she disappears down the street. If I was a betting man, I'd say that was a look of jealousy gracing her beautiful face, but why?

The waiting room has cleared out by now and it's just her and me in the empty space. She avoids looking my direction at all costs and it's actually kinda cute.

"So, you're the other half of the Blake puzzle, huh?" I ask, breaking the silence.

"Huh? Oh! Yeah. That's me. Twin B." She scoffs lightheartedly. "I've heard Everett talk about you before. You guys served together before all of this, right?" She asks, leaning forward in her seat intently.

"Yeah, we spent a few nights snuggled in the sandbox together. Your brother is a dumbass, but a great one. I'm glad to know him," I tell her.

She smiles softly at my response. "Yeah, he has that effect on most people. Magnetic personality and all." She says, waving her hand through the air. "He got the personality and the good looks. I got everything else," she says jokingly.

I stare back at her intensely. Does she really not know she's a knockout? "If anybody got the looks there, it definitely wasn't him." I tell her and I think I hear a gasp. I lock eyes with her from across the room and I can tell she's surprised by my words. She really doesn't know how gorgeous she is. I wouldn't mind showing her exactly what I see in her. If only she wasn't Everett's sister. I can see the blush staining her cheeks from here and I love the way it looks on her. Knowing I'm the one who put it there does something to me I can't quite explain. I flex my hands behind the desk so she can't see the way she's affecting me.

"How long do you think he's gonna be?" She asks, her voice sounding sleepier by the second. She yawns, stretching her arms over her head and rolling her neck. Watching the slow motions of her body has my dick growing thicker in my jeans. I adjust myself to ease some discomfort and step around the desk.

"You're welcome to head over to the house whenever you want to. I'm not sure how much he's got left, but it could be a few more hours." I tell her, reaching under the desk for the spare set of keys Everett had made for her. "Do you know how to get there?"

She's looking at me wide-eyed, but silent. I don't think I said anything to cause this reaction. Maybe she's irritated with her brother for taking so long? Who knows with women.

"You said 'the house', not his house. Do you live there too?" She asks, looking shocked. I huff out a breath and look up to the ceiling, exasperated by Everett's lack of details.

"Yeah, I do. I'm guessing Ev didn't share that with you by the look on your face." She immediately schools her features, her face suddenly void of emotion. "Is that gonna be a problem?" I snap a little more aggressively than I intend to. I must be getting tired, too.

"No! Of course not. I mean, it's your house too. I'm just grateful for the hospitality." She says looking worried "Oh, god! He made sure this was okay with you, right?! He's notorious for acting without thinking. I can't imagine he would just spring a whole person on you, but you really never know with my brother. I'm so sorry if he didn't. I'm sure I could find a hotel or something if I need to." She's practically panting with anxiety and I don't think she realizes she's gotten up and made her way across the room to stand right next to me.

Looking down at her, I grab her shoulders softly to steady her breathing, and a bolt of electricity shoots through my arms at the touch. She lets out a small gasp and I know she felt it too. Quickly removing my hands and holding them up in surrender, I take a step back.

"Calm down, sunshine. He made sure he told me everything before he even offered you the room. It's fine by me." Did I really just call her sunshine? Am I fucking fourteen? I can't help it though. The light surrounding her is blinding, but she seems oblivious to it. I try my best to soften my tone and be reassuring. "I can see why he calls you Sparky," I laugh, and the blush stains her cheeks and chest again. God, that's a sight to behold.

She runs her palms down her thighs nervously. "Well, I have the address that he gave me, so I'm sure I could find my way. I'll just grab the keys from him and head out," she says shyly, looking anywhere but my face.

"I've got your set right here," I hold them up in my palm, "and I'm getting ready to head out now so you can follow me if you want to." This is not a good idea. I already don't trust myself around this woman.

"Okay, if you're sure. I am exhausted, so I really don't wanna wait a few more hours for him." She looks relieved as she runs her hands across her hair, catching the fly-aways that have fallen out of her messy bun.

"Yeah, let me just lock up my shit and tell Ev we're

leaving. Be right out." I watch her walk out the front door and climb into the driver's seat of her cherry red Jeep Wrangler.

I knock on the door frame of Everett's station, and he snaps his attention to me. His client is finishing a chest piece that's been stretched out over several sessions, so this should be the last.

"Hey, your sister is looking pretty beat and I'm done for the night. You cool if we head out? She's gonna follow me back to the house, and I don't mind helping her unload shit." I tell him.

"Yeah, dude, that would be awesome. I feel shitty that I'm tied up here, but I've had this appointment booked for months and we're both ready to be done. Just tell her to leave any of the bigger shit she brought locked in the trailer and I'll take care of it tomorrow." He tells me dismissively, already turning back to focus on his client.

I lock up my station and grab my helmet and jacket from the table in the kitchen. I take a quick look over the schedule for tomorrow and head out the front door, locking it behind me. I can see Ember with her head laying against her steering wheel and it's pretty damn adorable. I tap lightly on the window, not trying to scare her, but she startles awake, immediately looking around like a scared deer. Once she sees me, her shoulders relax and she rolls the window down.

"You ready?" She nods. "Ok, follow me. When we get

there, you pull up all the way into the garage and we'll lock your shit up so we don't have to unload everything tonight."

She gives me a nod and a small smile as I walk over to my bike. Swinging my leg over the seat of my Harley Softail, I drop my ass onto the cool leather and rev the engine. The sound of the pipes is always music to my ears. I pull out onto the road, hoping the drive will clear my mind of thoughts of the green-eyed beauty behind me.

seven

A HARLEY. Of course, he rides a damn Harley. Could he be any more of the poster child for a sexy bad boy? I must be hallucinating at this point from exhaustion. I follow closely behind him through town and into a quieter suburban area. I laugh at the rows of colorful townhouses, imagining Everett and Elijah touring them together when they first got here. Both are what you would call "manly" men and I'm sure whoever helped them got a good laugh from it.

We pull up to a light blue colored two-story building and Eli waves, motioning for me to pull into the garage. I squeeze my Jeep as far forward as I can, hoping the trailer isn't sticking outside the door. I see Eli walking up behind the Jeep giving me the thumbs up, so I put it in park and grab the small duffle bag from the backseat that has my essentials in it.

"This all you need for tonight?" He asks, pointing to my bag.

"Yeah, I travel light and I can always come get anything else I need in the morning," I answer with a yawn. He nods and leads the way to the side door after closing and locking the garage. I take a second to take in my surroundings before going inside. This building is obviously old, I would guess late 1800s, but it's been remodeled and well maintained. The landscaping isn't overgrown or neglected, the way many would assume for two bachelors living here.

The door opens into a narrow mudroom where Eli hangs his keys on a hook by the door and takes his heavy leather boots off, pushing them under a bench. I sit down on the bench and untie my vans. This must be something important to Elijah, because Everett has never cared about making a mess.

"I like things to be clean. Less work to keep up with." Elijah says, as if he can read my mind. "It took a few years to train your brother, but eventually he learned," He says with a smirk and I laugh, imagining the two at odds over who's going to clean what over the years.

We walk down the short hallway and into the main living space. The kitchen, dining room, living room, and entry way are all open, no walls separating the areas. A large bar-height island is all that stands between the living room and kitchen. I look around at the masculine but tidy room around me and instantly feel at home.

Something about the fact that you could watch TV while you're cooking in the kitchen or having a conversation with somebody who's in the living room gives me major "Friends" vibes and I love it.

"The master bedroom is down here in that back corner," he points to the closed door just past the entryway, "the other two bedrooms and bathrooms are upstairs. We flipped for the master when we moved in and Everett won, so he's there and I'm upstairs. Honestly, all the rooms are big enough to be suites and each has their own bathroom, so you won't have to worry about sharing."

I breathe a sigh of relief at that fact, knowing the chaos that ensued when Everett and I shared a bathroom back home.

"Consider anything here yours. All I ask is if you eat the last of something, write it on the board on the fridge so we can restock."

I nod my head, making a note to find a market tomorrow and pick up a few of my favorite snacks. We stand in comfortable silence for a long minute, both surveying the space around us. Eli picks up my duffle bag from the bar and heads towards the stairs, leaving me with no choice but to follow.

"There's not a lot left to show you up here," he says, motioning around the loft space, "built-in desk over there that we both sometimes use for sketching because it gets great natural light in the middle of the day. But we both have our own drafting tables in our rooms, so you're welcome to it for whatever it is you do. Everett mentioned something about you working for a publishing company?" He asks, and my eyes light up at the mention of my job.

"Yes! I'm so excited to start. It's an indie publishing company that works with independent authors to help them get on their feet when they're starting out. They help connect the authors with marketing resources, bookshops, and even other similar authors to help them grow their reader-base. I was lucky enough to see a flyer for the position at the coffee shop my friend Kelsea worked at back in Durham. A paid internship right after graduation is almost unheard of." He looks at me as if he's hanging on my every word, which surprises me. I thought for sure he would be bored by now with all my book talk.

"It sounds like an excellent opportunity," he says, shaking his head, "but I'm sure luck had nothing to do with it. I'm sure you charmed them all until they just couldn't say no." he says with a soft smile.

I feel the heat rising into my cheeks and I know he's made me blush for the thousandth time tonight. Such a small compliment shouldn't affect me this way, but I find myself thinking I'm glad he finds me charming. I look away, trying to contain my embarrassment, but he reaches a calloused hand out to softly grasp my chin. The same jolt of electricity I felt before at the shop races through my skin. He forces my eyes back to his, letting out a small groan when our gazes collide.

"Don't hide that beautiful blush from me. It's hot as fuck, Sunshine." He says, his gaze searing through me like a hot poker. His forwardness makes my core clench and I pull my bottom lip between my teeth.

He quickly drops his hand as if I've burned him, taking a step back. The distance between us suddenly feels like the Grand Canyon. A flood of confusion and disappointment washes over me. Before I can process what just happened, he's already turning around and moving towards another closed door.

He continues the tour as if nothing happened. "The door down that way is mine. Yours is right here." He swings open the door closer to the stairs, revealing a decent sized bedroom. No doubt my queen bed will look pretty small in the space, but I'm glad to see two large windows on the far wall. Having my own bathroom in a house full of boys also doesn't suck. He sets my duffle bag down on the air mattress in the corner, but before I can turn around to thank him, Eli is gone. The only noise I hear is the sound of his bedroom door closing with a little more force than necessary.

Choosing to ignore his mood swings, I change into my comfy sleep shorts, take off my bra, and crash hard.

eight

Ember

I GROAN as the morning light cuts across my face. I've gotta remember to get some curtains today when I go out. Looking down at my phone, the clock reads 9:45 am. Wow, I must have been tired as hell. I rarely sleep past 8, even after a night out with Kelsea. I swing my legs over the side of the air mattress, stretching my aching back. First thing on my list today is to get my bed put together. I can't take another night on that thing. Shuffling to the bathroom, I go about fulfilling my morning routine. Teeth brushed, face washed, and hair in a high pony, I make my way down the stairs. I can hear the guys joking back and forth in the kitchen about whose lines are better. I'm assuming that's some kind of tattoo lingo which is totally lost on me.

"He cooks," I say, causing both men to snap their

attention in my direction. Everett sits on a barstool with the paper in front of him while Elijah looks to be making French toast in a skillet on the stove.

"Well hello there, sleepyhead!" My brother snakes an arm around my shoulder and squeezes. "About fuckin' time you got down here. I was this close to waking your ass up to come enjoy my gourmet breakfast."

I look over at Eli, who rolls his eyes and turns back to the stove, flipping the toast before it burns. "Yeah Ev, you look like a real Gordon Ramsey in here, observing all and doing nothing." I jibe and I swear I hear Eli snickering.

"Hey, it's the thought that counts, babe. I *thought* you would love to survive through breakfast, so I dragged Eli's ass out of bed because you know this pretty face doesn't cook." Everett says with a shrug.

"Well, I guess I should thank you for thinking about me at all," I scoff.

Eli turns around with a serving tray piled high with thick slices of French toast and a mason jar with what looks to be maple syrup in it. Setting it down on the bar between my brother and me, he turns to retrieve plates from the cabinet behind him.

"Thank you, Elijah," I say, not meaning to sound so breathy. I see the muscles in his back tense and relax and he mumbles back a quick, "You're welcome."

Settling in my seat at the bar, I dig in to the delicious

breakfast in front of me. I've never been one to shy away from a good meal. Even when I was surrounded by sorority girls in the campus cafeteria, I never felt an ounce of shame eating an extra pancake or two. This French toast is unlike anything I've ever tasted on campus, though. Not only is he built like a fucking Greek god, but the man can cook, too. I let out a small moan as the bite melts in my mouth. A fork clattering to the counter top across from me breaks my food trance. Eli recovers quickly, but not before I feel the familiar heat of a blush creeping up my body. Remembering back to his rough hands on my face last night makes it that much worse. I shiver in my seat, my nipples tightening at the thought of his hands on my skin. My throat goes dry as I reach for the glass of water in front of me, gulping it down. Hearing Eli clear his throat, I look up to see him staring straight at my shirt. No, not my shirt. My very visible and hard nipples practically poking through the fabric of my white sleep shirt. I quickly cross my arms over my chest, but it's too late. He's already seen the effect he has on my body.

"Well, this was delicious. I'm gonna go change," I say in a rush, not giving either of them a chance to say anything before I'm halfway up the stairs and safely inside my room. I push my back against the door and slide down to the floor. Will there ever be a time when I don't completely embarrass myself in front of this man?

Most likely not. I'm gonna have to remember to wear a bra at all times around here.

I grab a towel and head for the bathroom to shower, hoping I can scrub the mortification from my skin. I turn the faucet halfway and suddenly water comes spraying out of the hole in the wall where the shower head used to be. I let out a shriek and I fumble for the handle to try to turn it off. Before I know it, both men are lumbering through my door like the house is on fire.

"What the hell?!" I hear Everett say while I'm still trying to stop the torrential downpour.

I feel a muscular arm come around my waist, dragging me out of the way and turning the faucet off. I turn to see a soaking wet Elijah staring at me and the personal wet t-shirt contest I'm having in my bathroom.

"Holy shit, Sparky. You broke the damn house already!" Everett says with a chuckle from behind Eli.

"I did not!! All I did was turn on the tap to take a damn shower!!" I throw back, putting my arms across my chest to cover my now completely transparent shirt.

"Pipe must be busted or something," Eli grumbles. "I don't think we've ever even used this bathroom. I didn't think to make sure everything was working okay."

"Well, I'm here to attest that everything is definitely not working okay," I say with a smirk, "but hey, at least the ceiling's clean." I shrug and point at the water dripping down all around us.

"Damn, I'm gonna go grab some extra towels." Everett says rushing downstairs.

"Such a silver lining thing to say, Sunshine." Eli gives me a magnificent smile. I wish I could take a picture of that smile and keep it forever.

"You should smile more often." I say without thinking. I see the fire in Eli's eyes blaze hotter as he watches me with a predatory gaze.

"Haven't had much to smile about lately. But I think that's turning around." He gives me a boyish grin that makes my heart drop into my stomach.

Our bubble is burst by my brother shoving towels between us. "Here, I could only find these two extra downstairs. We'll have to pick up a couple more today and call the landlord tomorrow to come fix this shit," Everett says, surveying the damage.

"I'll see what I can do with it. In the meantime, you're welcome to use mine," Eli says, surprising me.

"Oh, um, are you sure? I don't wanna impose or anything." I say, awkwardly clutching a towel to my chest.

"Well, you definitely don't wanna use mine, Sparky." Everett says, walking back downstairs. "You've lived with me before. You, of all people, know cleaning is my kryptonite. You'd be better off with the hose in the backyard," he jokes, but thinking back to a teenage Everett, I know he's not lying.

"Yeah, it's no problem. A girl has to shower, right? I'll

have to turn off the water in this room anyway, so you'll have to have somewhere to go." Eli sounds very calm and collected, making me wonder how many other women he's invited to use his bathroom. An unfamiliar pang of jealousy strikes through me. Where the hell did that come from? I've never been the jealous type, and he doesn't belong to me. But maybe I wish he did.

nine

Elijah

DID I just invite her to use my shower? Yeah, I think I did. I've never allowed a woman into my space before. I've never been interested in anyone long enough to bring them into my home, but here I am inviting Ember to share my bathroom like it's totally natural. But it does feel natural. Being next to her feels completely organic, like something is telling me that's where I'm supposed to be. I feel a pull to her I don't quite understand or want to acknowledge right now. Something in her eyes every time she looks at me tells me she feels it, too. What would Everett have to say about this, though?

Everett has been my best friend for four years now. He and a few others joined our unit straight out of bootcamp. They dropped us all in the desert, experienced or not, gave us guns and left us to clean up the mess. That kind of circumstance creates a bond between people that most don't understand. Those are men I would die for and I know they would do the same for me. Maybe that's why these feelings stirring in me feel like a betrayal. What would he think if he knew the things I've been thinking about his sister? He's always told me stories of how protective he's been over the years. According to him, she's always had a propensity to attract total douchebags. I'm far from a frat boy, but I don't think I'm the guy anybody would want around their sister.

I scoop the sopping wet towels off the floor and toss them into the tub. Ember is standing awkwardly in the doorway and it's so damn cute I can hardly look away. Her hair is up in that sexy messy bun girls always do and her white tee is practically see-through at this point. I stand and take a step closer to her, almost like the magnetic pull is too much for me to resist. I can hear her breathing pick up as I brace my arms on the door frame on either side of her. The air surrounding us thickens, and I can see that sexy red blush creeping up her neck.

"You might wanna grab a new shirt," my voice comes out gravelly and the tension in my body has me flexing my shoulders to try to alleviate the strain. My eyes burn a path all the way down her sexy as sin body, coming back to lock on to the perfect peaks of her nipples pushing against the fabric of her t-shirt. She lets out a small gasp and clutches the towel to her chest tighter, looking up into my eyes. I swear this woman can see straight into my soul. If it were anyone else, I'd be scared shitless. But somehow with Ember, I almost want her to see those parts of me.

"I don't know, I'm kinda ok with this one," She says, shrugging as if she's unconcerned. But the nervousness in her eyes betrays her true feelings. I reach out and brush a loose strand of her hair behind her ear and her eyes flutter closed.

"Look at me, Sunshine." I say, my tone tight and demanding. Her eyes snap to mine instantly and I can see the lust flaming in them. She likes a little alpha in a man, that's obvious. If that's what she wants, I'm more than happy to oblige. "Don't hide from me," I say with authority. "I'll always find you."

"What is this, Elijah? Tell me I'm not the only one who feels whatever this is," she says, surprising me. I didn't expect such a forward question from her, but I appreciate a direct woman.

"I honestly don't know." I grasp her chin in my hands and stroke the soft skin of her cheek. "But I know I wanna find out. And I'm not sure how much longer I can go without knowing how your lips taste," I tell her, my face only inches from hers.

"So, find out," she says in a whisper. I can feel her shallow breaths brushing across my lips and I can't take it anymore. The tight wire I've been walking snaps and I crash my lips down onto hers. Threading my fingers through her hair, tugging just enough to tilt her head back, I take the kiss deeper and deeper. She tastes better than I could ever have imagined. Like sunshine and cinnamon, a spicy sweet mixture that intoxicates me and I already know I could never get enough. I nip at her bottom lip, causing her to gasp, and I take my opportunity to slide my tongue into her mouth. She lets out a small moan, rising up on her tiptoes, her arms sliding up and around my shoulders. I push her back against the bathroom wall, taking and taking anything she's willing to give me. God, this woman could become an addiction stronger than any drug. Just the feel of her skin brushing against mine is enough to make my cock swell hard as a fucking rock. My grey sweats do nothing to conceal my body's reaction to this seductress and I don't even fucking care. I want her to know exactly how she affects me. The feeling of her nails dragging across my scalp makes me groan in pure satisfaction.

The repetitive pinging of a cell phone drags us away from each other. We're both panting, staring at each other, the fire in both our eyes barely banked. She reaches for me again, only to be stopped by the sound of her phone ringing from across the room. She closes her eyes, breaking our connection. Pulling away, she walks to her nightstand and answers the phone.

"Hey Kelsea, what's up? Isn't it kinda early for you? It's before noon," she laughs, obviously comfortable with whoever is on the other end. Watching the sun hit her face through the window, I take a minute to appreciate just how beautiful she is. Her soft feminine features look so delicate, but I don't think she's easily broken. I'm dying to know every facet of this beautiful creature in front of me.

"What?!" I immediately hear the panic in her voice and I come closer to try to hear the other side of her conversation. "How did he even get in, Kelsea? I left the next day. He didn't even know I was gone." Her voice is shaking and I can feel the fear radiating off of her in waves. "Ok, just be careful, please. Don't do anything insane, even if you want to. It won't help, babe," a tear rolling slowly down her cheek. She swipes it away quickly, but I know whatever is going on here is obviously tearing her up. "I love you too, girl. Please be safe," she wipes at the moisture around her eyes and hangs up the phone.

"You wanna tell me what the hell that was about?" I ask, with confusion and worry. She turns her back to me, but the shaking in her shoulders shows me she's crying. I cross the small distance left between us and wrap my arms around her, not giving her the chance to pull away. "Hey, it's okay. Whatever it is, it's gonna be fine. Shhh."

"I shouldn't have come here," she whispers so softly I almost don't hear her.

"What do you mean?" I try to push for any hint of information she's willing to give me.

"It's not safe to be around me," she tries to push me

away and I loosen my grip, but don't let go. "This can't happen, Elijah. It's not a good idea."

"You don't know that." I know I shouldn't argue with her about this because she's probably right. This could be a huge mistake. But something in her eyes is so familiar to me. That look of someone trying to escape is one I know all too well. I see it in my own eyes every time I look in the mirror. Lost souls, the both of us.

I kiss her hair softly as she clings to me. I don't know what just happened during that call, but at that moment, I decide I'll protect her from anything. That realization rocks me to my core. Typically, a thought like that would scare the shit out of me. But I'm already hooked on this woman after just one taste.

ten

Ember

THE EXCITEMENT I felt moments ago with Elijah's lips on mine is extinguished in an instant. Hearing the fear and panic in Kelsea's voice wracks me with guilt and despair. This is my fault and anything that happens after this will be my fault, too. Elijah's powerful arms are wrapped around my shoulders, and I wish I could stay here forever. I was shocked when he kissed me, but we've been dancing around each other since we first locked eyes. I feel his hands rubbing my back as I bury my face deeper into his chest. I can't stand crying in front of other people. It's a show of weakness people can use to exploit you. But here, in this moment with Eli, I somehow know he would never do that to me. I feel safe falling apart just a little, believing he would catch me.

"Tell me what's going on, Ember," He says, his voice laced with genuine concern. I could lie. I could make up some silly explanation for my breakdown. But something tells me he would see right through it. And surprisingly, I don't want to lie to him. I don't want to feel alone in this anymore.

"That was my best friend back in Durham. I asked her to go by my old place to grab the few things I left behind and leave the keys for the landlord. She said when she got there the police were everywhere. The landlord told her someone broke into my old apartment and trashed the place. She said it looked like somebody went through it with a sledgehammer, destroying everything in their path." He listens intently, a tick in his jaw telling me this is upsetting him.

"Go on. Obviously, this wasn't random if they destroyed your shit instead of stealing it." He says discerningly.

"No, I know it wasn't random. I know exactly who did this." My eyes fall to the floor, shame and guilt flooding my system. If I hadn't been stupid enough to fall for Justin, none of this would have happened. Elijah puts a finger under my chin and brings my eyes back up to his. "Tell me, Ember. Now." His tone steeped in authority.

"I had a boyfriend back at school. We dated for a while when I was in my second year there. I thought he was an okay guy. He didn't really blow me away, but he was decent company. But he had another side to him I didn't know about. The first time he put his hands on me was the last time." I say the last part quietly and I can see the rage building in his eyes.

"He put his hands on you?" He asks, his voice dripping with venom. His fists clench and unclench at his sides, and I can tell he's pissed. "Why didn't you call Everett? I know he would have told me if something like this happened and we both would have been there in a heartbeat to beat this guy's ass."

"I didn't think it would escalate the way it has. I told him we were done the day after our fight and he didn't argue. He tried reaching out a few times, but I just assumed he wanted me back. I didn't think he was dangerous, Elijah." I say, straightening my spine. I know I should have said something to my brother, but I'm not incapable of taking care of myself. Elijah's alpha male bullshit is hot, but I won't be made to feel like some helpless damsel. "It didn't worry me until right before I left. I got a note from him that really freaked me out and I got out of there as fast as I could."

"The night you called Everett and asked if you could come down early, is that why?" He asks and I nod.

"I packed all my shit that I could fit into the trailer, and I left the next day. I guess you could say I ran, but he had no idea when or where I was going, so I just wanted to get out of there" I want to escape the scrutiny I feel under his gaze. I'm sure he thinks I'm such a fucking idiot for not going to the cops or telling Everett, and honestly, I can't disagree with him. I should have spoken up. But hindsight's twenty-twenty.

His features soften. I can tell he's still enraged, but doing his best to control his emotions. "You have to tell Everett, Sunshine," he says, reaching for my hand and giving it a reassuring squeeze. "He needs to know what's really going on."

I huff out a breath, pulling my hand away from his. "No, Elijah, I don't need to tell Everett. I'm not some meek little girl who needs her brother to take care of her. Justin has no idea where I am. I don't have any reason to believe he would come after me. I'm sure he was just pissed he couldn't get to me anymore," I say, placing my hand on my hip, hoping I look intimidating. Unfortunately, I don't think that's gonna happen.

"Ember, you have to tell him. This asshole is obviously a fucking whack job. He broke into your place! Who fucking knows what he would have done if you had still been there!" A cool shiver runs through my body, my eyes going wide. I know he's right. What if I had been alone in my apartment when Justin broke in? What would he have done? I don't even want to think about that or I'll just crawl back into bed and never leave. Eli puts his hand on my hip, pulling me closer to him. He places a hand on the side of my neck, leaning my head back so he can look me in the eyes. "He has to know what could come knocking at our door. It's not fair to keep him in the dark. Especially when it comes to your safety." He says, and I drop my forehead onto his chest.

"I know," I grumble. "He's gonna freak the fuck out."

"He might, yeah, but not at you. He's a rational guy, and he loves you. You can't blame a guy for wanting to protect you." He says, his gaze piercing through mine, causing my core to clench. I can't help it when he looks at me that way, like I'm something precious.

"I guess that's not the only thing we need to tell him." I say, giving him a small grin.

"I don't think that's a good idea. Not right now. Your safety is what's most important, and I don't think adding anything else into the mix is a good thing." He says, taking a step back from me. I instantly feel the weight of his loss and a wave of disappointment flood over me. Then rage and annoyance overpower my emotions.

"So, what, I'm supposed to be your dirty little secret? Or was what just happened here just insignificant to you?" I say, trying and failing to control my anger. He reaches out to try and calm me, but I step back. "Just go, Elijah. You don't need to let me down easy. I'm a big girl." I cross my arms over my chest, completely shutting him out.

He looks at me, his eyes pleading for my understanding. But I can't think rationally right now, and his rejection stings. "I'll go for now, but you need to tell him, Ember. Tell him or I will," He says, walking out of my room and into his own, slamming the door.

eleven

Elijah

I MARCH STRAIGHT into my bathroom, turning the shower as cold as possible and stripping out of my clothes. Walking under the spray, I let the frigid water wash over my skin, attempting to calm my throbbing erection. I know seeing Ember pissed off shouldn't be such a turn on, but damn it is. She's sexy as fuck when that fire flares in her eyes and I know it could burn me down. The thought of her lips on mine, the taste of cinnamon exploding on my tongue, has my dick aching already. Grasping my shaft tightly, I try to ease the ache. I pump my fist slowly at first, then harder and faster, already feeling the familiar tingle building in my spine. Fighting with a woman has never been a turn on for me. But with Ember, I'm not sure she could do anything that wouldn't turn me on. I imagine how amazing it would feel if it was her mouth wrapped around my cock, her small hands pumping faster and faster. My release comes faster that I expect and I have to brace myself on the shower wall to keep my knees from giving out. Jet after jet of thick cum coats the tile floor, washing down the drain. I don't think I've ever needed relief so badly in my life. This woman has me wound up tight.

Wiping a hand down my face, I try and fail to shake the thought of her from my mind. I know she thinks she doesn't need anybody's protection, but she's wrong. She doesn't know what crazy fuckers like that are capable of. I understand why she didn't want to say anything, but damn. It's really a matter of pride. Her safety is more important than her ego in this situation. She's not a fucking mind reader. She couldn't have known how big of a prick that guy would turn out to be. Making her realize this isn't her fault will be a challenge, though.

I step out of the shower and wrap a towel around my waist. Walking into my bedroom, I lay back on the edge of my bed, staring at the ceiling. I know I said I would tell Everett if she didn't. And I almost feel like bro-code obligates me to tell him about this. Then again, bro-code probably says I should tell him I was just jacking off in the shower to the thought of his sister, and I definitely know I can't do that.

When Ember referred to herself as a dirty little secret, it burned deep in my chest. I knew she was pissed. That wasn't how I meant it to go down, but maybe that's for the best. I could see the pain etched across her face when she told me to go, and I know I'm the one who caused it. Telling Everett about whatever is happening between us will only complicate a situation that's already fucked. A woman like her should never be hidden in the background, but her safety is the priority.

I dress quickly and head downstairs. Ember is sitting at the bar, dressed and ready to go out. Everett is leaning up against the counter, staring at her intently. I approach them both slowly and she turns to look at me. The anger in her eyes is burning a hole through me. Everett turns his gaze to me over her shoulder, his brows knitting together in confusion.

"Ok, who saw who naked?" He says, and the blood drains from my face. "Well, I can tell from the look on both of your faces that something happened. Twin telepathy, remember, Sparky?" He says, tapping his finger against his temple. "So spill. What the hell is going on?"

"Nobody saw anybody naked, Everett. Jesus, can you try to be a normal person for like 30 seconds, please?" Ember says, rolling her eyes.

"Okay, okay. But who wants to see who naked?" He smirks and Ember throws a magazine at him. He catches it, laughing at her obvious embarrassment. I don't think I've ever seen a family dynamic like the one they share. They both seem so attuned to each other's thoughts and emotions, it almost makes me jealous. My relationship with my sister is great, but nothing like this.

"Come on Ember, you know you want a piece of that!" He says pointing at me and giving me a wink. Now it's my turn to roll my eyes at him.

"That doesn't want a piece of me, Everett," She mumbles quietly, gesturing my way. I'm floored by her revelation. There's no way to keep our encounter from him now. His eyes rake over her, trying to discern if she's serious, I assume. Then they lock on me.

"That's not what I said, Ember," my tone is harsh but what the fuck? We just talked about this and now she's laying it out there for him like it's nothing. "What I said was there are more important things than what I want right now, aren't there?" She shrinks back into her seat, turning her eyes intently to the bar top.

"Okay, somebody talk. Now!" Everett snaps and I see Ember jump on her stool. I watch her intently and she remains quietly focused on her hands.

"Look, here's what it is, Ev. Elijah and I kissed and it was amazing but then Kelsea called and told me Justin broke into my old apartment and Eli thinks he's a psycho and he thinks you're gonna be pissed about us kissing even though it's really not your business because we're both adults," She says, the words coming out rushed and chaotic. She takes a deep breath, slumping back into the chair. I look over to Everett and see him staring at me, his emotions guarded.

"Well, that wasn't exactly how this was supposed to play out, but too late now, I guess." I say, huffing out a breath and sitting down next to Ember at the bar.

"We've never kept secrets, Everett. I'm not gonna start now. I'm sorry if you're pissed off, but I won't lie to you." Her gaze shifts from him to me and back again.

"Well. Okay then." He grabs his cigarettes and walks out onto the back deck. He closes the French doors behind him and Ember and I are left alone together. The silence is palpable between us, tensions growing thicker by the second

"I'm sorry, Elijah. But I won't lie to my brother. I've never kept a single detail of my life from him and he hasn't kept anything from me. I won't start now." She says, looking down at her hands in her lap.

"You really think I don't want you, Ember?" I ask her. She looks up into my eyes, some of the tension relaxing in her features. "I'd be damn lucky to call you mine. I just think dealing with this situation with your ex is more important."

"Well, what about what I think? I think Justin has taken enough from me. I don't think you're something I'm willing to give up yet," she says, her gaze boring into mine. I don't think I've ever had somebody look at me the way she does. Like she wants me, the real me. Sure, women have told me they want me before. But what they really want is to take a walk on the wild side before they go back to their safe southern-belle lives.

"Well, I guess the cat's outta the bag now, huh? We'll see where the chips fall," I tell her, putting my hand over hers and stroking gently. She smiles over at me and I know I'll do just about anything I have to do to keep that smile on her face as long as I can.

twelve

I GET the feeling that Elijah doesn't think he's good enough to be wanted. I don't know why he thinks that, but I understand having that kind of insecurity. I've always felt like there wasn't anything special enough about me for someone to want me. When Eli looks at me, I want to be that special.

His fingers are still laced with mine when Everett comes back inside and he doesn't attempt to pull them away. Everett rubs his hand down his face and props himself up against the counter.

"So, this is how it's gonna be, huh?" He asks, pointing to our joined hands. Elijah and Everett are locked in some kind of stare down and I'm not sure what will happen next.

"Yeah, brother. I think this is how it's gonna be," Eli says, never breaking eye contact or releasing my hand.

Everett nods slowly, absorbing the weight of our decision. His gaze swings to me and I give him a nod of agreement. I want to see where this goes with Elijah, and I'm willing to take the risk.

"Well, E, I hope you're ready for it, I guess. Because she's annoying as fuck. Especially when she sets her mind to something." Everett says, his tone sounding completely serious but I see the humor in his eyes. I roll my eyes, scoffing at his accusation that I'm the annoying twin. Elijah lets out a riotous laugh and kisses the back of my hand.

"I think I can handle her, but I appreciate the warning," he says.

"As long as I don't have to hear you 'handling her', then I'm cool," Everett says, and I instantly feel my body heat with embarrassment.

"EVERETT WAYNE! You did not just say that!" I say, burying my face in my hands. I hear them both laughing as if my embarrassment is entertaining to them.

My brother's face turns sombre and I can see the wheels turning in his head. Now that the shock of me and Elijah has worn off, he's ready to address my confession about Justin. "Out with it, Ember. What's going on with Justin? I thought he was history years ago," he questions.

"Yeah, I thought so, too. We had a rough break up, but I hadn't heard from him in so long. Right before I left Duke, he sent me a creepy note about how we could be together now that I had graduated and could devote my time to him. Apparently, he had been following me around campus, taking pictures of me and Kelsea together and stuff like that. It just made me feel uneasy, which is why I asked if I could come here sooner. He had no idea when I was leaving or where I was going, so I just figured it was best to get gone as soon as possible." I brace my hands on the bar, the whole situation giving me a headache.

"Well, what the hell, Ember? This guy obviously can't take a hint! Taking pictures of you? That's creepy as fuck! Why didn't you tell me about this before?" Everett says, pacing the kitchen.

"I don't know, Ev. I'm fucking embarrassed. I should've known he was a douchebag from the beginning, and I wouldn't even be in this mess." I say, dropping my head into my hands. The sting of tears burns my eyes and I will them away. I won't waste any more tears on Justin and I definitely won't let them fall in front of these men that surely think I'm an incompetent judge of character at this point.

"That's not the end of it, Ember. Tell him the rest," Eli says, brushing his hand across my shoulders reassuringly. I give him my best go to hell look for ratting me out and brace myself for my brother's reaction to the rest of the story.

"Kelsea called to tell me that somebody broke into my apartment back at Duke. Apparently, what little stuff

I left behind was destroyed along with some damage to the apartment itself. She said the cops were everywhere, and the landlord was freaking out. Kelsea was the only person who knew I left, Everett. Justin wouldn't have known I was gone. I don't even want to think about what would have happened if I had still been there." I say the last part quietly, mostly to myself.

The sound of glass shattering against the wall has me flinching in my seat, and tears instantly well up in my eyes. Once his temper flares, it's enough to burn down the entire world. The glass that was in Everetts hands moments ago now lays in pieces on the floor next to the back door.

"FUCK!" He screams, his fists balled up, ready for a fight. He's pacing violently around the kitchen, barely keeping his anger in check. He's always been a hothead, quick to anger and hard to bring back down. That's probably why I never told him I was having problems to begin with. He always stood up for me, with his voice or his fists, when we were kids. I didn't want to put him in that position again. I let the tears fall from my eyes, not attempting to stop them or wipe them away.

"Ember, when you say you had a rough break up, what do you mean, exactly?" He asks me and I immediately look away, knowing he'll see the truth I'm trying to hide. Eli catches my gaze and I can see the anger burning behind his eyes, too. I want to say something to explain this whole situation away. I open my mouth and no words come out. The thought of my brother being disappointed in me is overwhelming, and I don't know if I could handle it.

"He put his hands on her," Elijah says, his tone ferocious. Part of me feels elated that Elijah feels this protective of me. I only wish he didn't have to.

"Are you fucking kidding me?" Everett says, a sinister tone in his voice that I barely recognize. He looks up at me and I nod slowly, the tears continuing to fall.

"I left as soon as it happened, Everett. Kelsea helped me kick him out after I told him we were done. I made sure I told security and my professors what happened. I did my best to protect myself." I plead my case, already knowing he won't accept that reasoning no matter what I say.

"Except you didn't, Ember. Because 'doing everything' would have included you picking up the damn phone and calling me. Giving me a chance to protect you and beat the shit out of this fuckwad would have been doing everything," He says, his voice raising until he's practically screaming at me.

"Ok, ok, let's calm down," Eli interjects "your sister isn't the one to blame here and making her feel like shit isn't gonna do anything but piss everybody off, Ev." I manage to give him a small smile for coming to my defense.

Everett lets out a heavy sigh, running his hands through his hair and locking them behind his head.

"You're right. I'm sorry, Sparky." He comes around the bar and wraps his arms around me. I cling to him like my life depends on it and let my tears fall freely. He strokes my hair gently, reassuring me everything will be fine. "I'll never let anyone hurt you again, Ember. You're safe here with us," he says with confidence, and I believe him. Over the past 22 years of our lives, he has always protected me, and I know he would do anything for me. If nothing else, at least I'm sure of that.

thirteen

Elijah

AFTER EMBER'S REVELATION, we all need some time to calm down and cool off. Everett grabbed the keys to his bike and took off. I know he has enough sense not to let his anger affect his driving, but I still told him to be careful. Walking past Ember's room, I see her sitting against her headboard with her knees pulled up to her chest. I knock and she wipes her face quickly, trying to conceal her tears.

"Hey, how you feeling?" I ask, sitting on the end of her bed. I take a second to look around her room. She's already made herself at home here over the last few hours and I love that.

She laughs sarcastically, "Oh, I'm just delightful, just a ray of fucking sunshine over here." She plasters on a fake smile, tears still rolling down her cheeks. I reach over and catch them before they fall. Her eyes close at the feeling of my hand on her face and she lets out a relaxed sigh. "How can you do that?" she asks.

"Do what?" I reply, confused.

"Make me feel so relaxed with just one touch," she says, her hand reaching up to cover mine against her cheek. "It's like all the weight I'm carrying just melts away as soon as you touch me."

"Well, if that's all it takes, I'm more than happy to touch you all you want," I say, giving her my best seductive smile and she laughs.

"You're such a man. I'm trying to be sweet and all you can think about is getting in my pants," she says, humor in her voice. The sound of her laugh makes me smile wide. "There's that smile again," she says, "you could really knock a lady out with that sight."

"Why do you think I'm always such an asshole? Gotta do something to keep the ladies off of me," I say, flexing my shoulders and she rolls her eyes.

"In all seriousness Ember, you know we won't let anything happen to you, right?" I ask, my tone soft but serious. She gives me a small smile and crawls over to sit next to me. I haul her into my lap and she lets out a small squeal. She wraps her arms around my neck, and I place my hands on either side of her face. "We will protect you, Sunshine. He'll never touch you again," I tell her with conviction. She brings her lips down to mine, kissing me softly at first. I flick my tongue out across her lips and she lets out a soft moan that I swear I can feel all the way through my dick. It grows harder against my zipper, and I pull her closer. Kissing her deeper, I give her everything she needs right now. She grinds her ass down against my throbbing shaft, and I growl. She lets out a wicked, seductive little laugh, and I know she's doing this on purpose. Little tease. But there's no way in hell I'm gonna stop her. We continue making out like a couple of horny teenagers, both of us ravenous for the other. I don't think I've ever wanted a woman as badly as I want her. She threads her hands through my hair, and the sting of her nails against my scalp has me ready to explode. I pull back a little, gasping for breath. I'm hard as a fucking rock for this woman.

"Em, we have to stop. If we don't, I'm gonna embarrass myself here," I say with a laugh, gesturing to the bulge in my jeans.

"But do we have to? Because I really don't want to." She whispers in my ear, kissing a path up my neck. It's sexy as fuck when a woman knows what she wants and takes it. I have no doubt Ember knows what she wants.

"Unless you want your brother to come in at any minute since the door is wide open, then yeah. We have to stop," I say, picking her up off my lap and setting her on her feet in front of me. She gives me a pouty look like I've just taken away her favorite toy and it's so damn adorable. I stand, adjusting myself to alleviate the ache. Bending down to give her a chaste kiss on the forehead, I can see that makes her happy. I make a mental note to do that as often as possible just to see that beautiful smile.

I finally take a minute to survey her room. I can see touches of her personality all over her space now that she's unpacked all of her stuff. The cozy reading chair in the corner has at least 3 printed manuscripts laying in the seat and a fuzzy black blanket draped over the back. My eyes stop on the giant pile of clothes piled in front of the closet door and I look at her quizzically. "Cleaning out the closet there?" I ask.

"Ughhh no. I don't have a stupid dresser," She says with a frustrated sigh. "I left it back in Durham because I couldn't fit it in the trailer. I just figured I'd go back for it one weekend. I guess that idea is shot."

Irritation bubbles under my skin at the thought of her personal things being destroyed like that. I push it down and choose to move on. "Well, I guess we need to go shopping then, huh?" I say, forcing some levity into my voice.

"You wanna go furniture shopping? I didn't think any man would be willing to subject themselves to such torture!" She says sarcastically.

"Hey, I'm not just any man, baby. You'd be amazed at the things I'm willing to subject myself to." I give her a wink and she rolls her eyes.

"Good lord, Elijah, you're incorrigible. Keep it in your pants." She says, grabbing her wallet and phone. "Fine, dresser shopping it is. But you're putting it together whenever we get back. I'm just here for supervision."

"That's a deal, Sunshine. I'll build it and you can sit your pretty ass on the bed and just admire my expert craftsmanship." I say with a smirk.

"Be careful there, honey. Your head might not fit inside my Jeep if you keep it up." She says, walking down the stairs. Something inside me lights up at her calling me honey. I've always hated being called a pet name, but with Ember, she could call me anything she wanted and I'd be happy. Something about the familiar way she says it, even though we've only known each other for a short time, makes my heart beat faster. Damn, this woman is gonna ruin me for sure.

fourteen

I'VE NEVER BEEN an expert in fine art, but I know what I think looks good and what I don't like. I can honestly say Elijah's ass in those grey sweats he has hung low on his hips is truly a work of art. I watch him as he moves effortlessly around my space, assembling the furniture he convinced me I needed yesterday. I have to admit he was right, though. I can't live out of a duffle bag or a pile of clothes on the floor forever. And the front-row seat to this show is worth every penny I spent today.

"I know you're lookin' at my ass, Sunshine. I have to say it's pretty objectifying," he says without turning around.

"Hey, I'm just making sure I'm giving my supervisor role everything I've got," I say, shrugging my shoulders. "I mean, what kind of woman would I be if I didn't give such fine artwork a thorough inspection?" I shoot him a wink and he laughs it off. I know Elijah is built like a god. I mean, I have eyes. What I didn't expect was for every other woman within a hundred miles to notice as well. I've never considered myself a jealous person. I'm confident enough in myself to know jealousy can be a toxic trait. But walking through the stores today with Eli, I found myself wanting to claw the eyes out of every woman who drooled over him. No matter where we went, women took notice. I can't blame them really, the man is obviously easy on the eyes. But for my eyes only would be nice.

"What's got you thinking so hard over there, Em?" He asks, dragging me from my thoughts. I quickly school my features, not wanting to sound clingy or crazy. I don't have any kind of claim over this man, and I don't want to scare him off.

"Nothing. Just thinking about how I'm gonna fill that sturdy dresser you've built. I think I'll have to go shopping," I say, wrinkling my nose. I've never been the girly type who enjoys shopping or hair and makeup shit. I preferred books and if a guy doesn't like me that way, then he doesn't deserve me.

"I don't know about that. Seems like something else is on your mind," he sees right through me, and it's honestly annoying. I fall back onto my bed and stare blankly at the ceiling. Suddenly, my view is obstructed by Eli hovering over me. He looks like he's doing pushups on top of me as his biceps flex, supporting his weight. "Tell me," he says, his lips slowly drawing closer to mine. I push up, trying to reach him, but he pulls back and holds himself just out of my reach. "Nope, not until you tell me what's on that beautiful mind," he smirks, playing on my weakness for those lips.

I huff out a breath, closing my eyes and throwing my arm over my face. "Fine! I was just thinking that I didn't really care much for the *extraordinary* amount of attention you attract from the ladies. They couldn't keep their eyes off you everywhere we went yesterday. It must get quite exhausting for you." I know I'm sporting a wonderful shade of red by now, but there's no hiding it. I feel him grab my arm gently and pull it off of my face, but I don't open my eyes.

"Look at me, Ember" he says. I crack one eye open and look up at his charming face. I can't help but smile when I see his saucy grin. "You telling me you're feeling a little jealous, Sunshine?" He says, humor lacing his tone. I can tell he finds this hilarious. Meanwhile, I'm just doing my best not to die from embarrassment.

"Fine! Yes! It that what you want to hear? I'm jealous. I don't like other women looking at you like they want to eat you for lunch. It makes me feel slightly stabby which I know sounds ridiculous because you don't belong to me and we haven't even discussed what this is or if this is like an exclusive thing and I don't -" my rambling is cut short by the feeling of his lips on mine. He slowly lowers his body, resting some of his weight on top of me, and it feels amazing. The pressure of his skin pressed against mine is comforting and arousing all at once. He kisses me softly at first, then deeper and harder, nipping at my bottom lip. I'm so lost in the feeling of contentment in his arms. I don't think I've ever felt this safe or wanted before. He slows his kisses, lazily teasing my lips.

"There's nothing wrong with feeling a little 'stabby', as you put it. What if I said I do belong to you, Ember?" he whispers. My eyes snap open and my brows knit together.

"You do?" I ask, surprised at his question. We haven't really put a label on what we're doing here. It's still so new and we've only spent a few days together. But I have to admit, when I'm with Elijah, it feels like I've known him for an entire lifetime. I've never felt such an intense passion or connection with anyone before, but he seems to have made up his mind already.

"Yeah, I think I do. I know we haven't really talked much about what's going on between us, but I want you to know I'm all in here. The first time I saw these beautiful green eyes, I knew I was done for. The way you say exactly what's on your mind, rambling when you're nervous, but speaking with conviction when you're passionate, it's like nothing I've ever seen before. I think you try to hide the parts of you that you think are weak from the world. But I see them, and they're just as beautiful as the rest of you. When I'm with you it's likes like my skin's on fire, burning to touch you. I look at you and I let myself have hope, which is something new for me. I never gave much thought to my future. I've been fine living day by day. But if there's a future for me, I hope to see you in it," he says, sounding completely sure of himself. I'm stunned by his openness to share his feelings with me. It's a rarity in any relationship. I take a deep breath, processing everything he's just told me and deciding where to go from here.

I place my hand softly on his cheek, loving the abrasive feeling of his stubble under my palm. "Well, that's good. Because I think I've belonged to you since the moment we met," I say with a wide smile. There's so much more I want to say to him, but my thoughts are an emotional, jumbled mess. I'll wait until I can tell him very clearly how I feel before I say anything. For now, I'm just happy to know we're in this together.

He runs his hand slowly from my hip up the side of my waist and back down again, causing a shiver to run down my spine. "So, it's settled then? You're my woman?" He growls into my ear, his thumb rubbing circles on my hipbone, driving me wild. I can't say I've ever been attracted to the alpha type. I've read about plenty of them in novels and always imagined how it would feel to be claimed by such a man. The desire in his eyes tells me he heard the small moan that escaped my throat.

"Yes," I say, feeling more sure of this decision than almost any other I've made in my life. "As long as you're mine," I say with a sexy grin, my hands threading through his long hair, hanging loose like a curtain around us. He smiles that perfect smile and I know I'm going to be ruined for anyone else.

"Of course, Sunshine. I'm all yours," he replies. I pull him down and crash my lips against his. He holds on tightly to my hips and rolls us over so I'm lying on top of him. Every nerve in my body is on fire as I raise up to straddle his hips. I grind my pelvic bone down onto his growing erection and I hear him growl. His left hand slides to the nape of my neck and he pulls me back down, attacking my lips in a frenzy. When he kisses me this way, I wonder if I've ever been properly kissed in my life. Elijah pours everything he has into these kisses and it leaves me breathless. I feel his hands slip under my shirt and burn a path across my skin. I raise up again quickly, pulling my shirt over my head, and he freezes. His eyes are roaming every inch of me like he's committing me to memory.

"God, you're so beautiful," he says, running his hands down my body. Goosebumps raise up on my skin under his scrutiny and I feel the heat rising up my neck. He runs one hand across my collarbone, down the swell of my breasts, and plucks my nipple through the thin lace covering it. I gasp at the shot of liquid heat that soars through me like a bolt of lightning. My core clenches at the thought of all the devilish things I want him to do with me. I feel my skin heat as he peruses by body and I reach behind me, unclasping my bra. I slide it down my arms and toss it on top of my new dresser. Under his gaze, I can already feel my nipples hardening into tight buds. He slides his rough, callused hands up my stomach and cups them gently, rolling my nipples between his fingers. I can't suppress the moan that rises from within me. I don't want to. He rolls us over again, lying me flat on my back. Slowly, he kisses down my jaw, across my neck, and down my chest, drawing my nipple into his mouth and sucking hard. My hands thread through his hair and hold him tightly in place. He nips and sucks, giving each side equal attention. My hips buck off the bed as he lavishes my overly sensitive breasts with attention. Wetness pools between my legs and I squeeze my thighs together to ease some of the ache. He kisses his way down my body, coming to a stop right above the waistband of my leggings. I lift my butt off the bed, giving him access to pull them down and off me. Before I can process the fact that I'm laying here under Elijah in nothing but my underwear, he hefts my leg up over his shoulder and his tongue darts out, sliding from my knee down to my center. The way he takes control of my body is driving me mad. I've never felt owned this way, but I love the heady feeling.

He stops his descent right above my panties and takes a deep breath. I watch his pupils dilate and I know he can smell my arousal. That is probably the most sensual thing I've ever seen and I'm surprisingly not the least bit embarrassed. I'm actually kinda turned on by it. I want him to know every inch of me intimately. I want him to crave me the way I do him. He kisses me softly over the lace of my panties and I heave a frustrated sigh. He's toying with me, and I know it. He slides my underwear down over my hips and parts my legs. I can feel my wetness dripping down my folds and I'm sure I'll be washing this comforter later.

"Every inch of you is perfection, Ember. I'll never get enough," he says, closing his eyes and breathing me in. "If you don't want this, if you're not ready, tell me to stop now, Sunshine. My control is hanging by a thread here." His gaze locks onto mine and I'm consumed by the fire burning there.

I smile lazily, enjoying the lust-filled high I'm riding right now. "Don't stop, Eli, please," I say, my voice trembling with need and desperation.

He takes my invitation greedily and lowers his mouth to my clit, sucking hard. I let out a loud moan as electricity floods every inch of my body. He feasts on me like a starving man and I can feel my climax already building like the waves in a hurricane. He groans against my skin and I arch my back, seeking more of his skillful tongue. "Sweet as fucking honey, baby. I knew you would taste incredible," he says, coming up for air before diving back in. He laps at me quickly, thrusting his tongue as deep inside me as he can before focusing his attention back on my clit. He pulls the bundle of nerves between his teeth and I cry out, coming so hard I see stars. My body falls back down to the bed, my heart racing in my chest as I come down from the sweetest high I've ever felt. Eli kisses his way back up my body before covering my mouth with his. I taste myself on his tongue and it's a spicy-sweet mixture of the two of us, delicious. He breaks our kiss, falling over onto the bed next to me with a wicked smile on his face.

"What are you smiling about over there?" I ask, my head still cloudy with adrenaline and lust.

"I'm doing that every fucking night, Ember. I've never tasted anything as sweet as your pussy. Damn, you pulled my hair so fucking hard I'm sure you drew blood," He says with a smirk and I'm flooded with embarrassment.

"Oh my god, I'm so sorry. I hope I didn't hurt you. I don't know what that was. You just made me feel so incredible I couldn't help it." I say, covering my face with my hands. I've never been aggressive in bed, but with Elijah, it's like I can't control myself. He plays my body like a skilled musician.

"Hey, stop. Don't overthink this, Sunshine," he pulls my hands into his and looks into my eyes, "You never have to be ashamed of anything that happens between us, Ember. It was sexy as fuck to watch you fall apart, knowing I'm the one who took you there." He pulls my hand to his lips and kisses my palm.

We lay in comfortable silence for a few long moments before the front door opens and closes, signaling Everetts return. I jump up from the bed and quickly pull my leggings back on. I feel like a teenager about to get caught by her parents. I throw my Duke University hoodie on, not bothering with my bra. My hands comb through my wild hair and pull it into a messy bun on top of my head. Elijah watches me intently from the bed with his head propped up on his hand. "What?" I ask, wondering what's running through his mind as he stares at me.

"Nothing, just glad you got that new dresser, babe," he says with a grin and I roll my eyes, pulling him up off the bed and dragging him downstairs for dinner.

fifteen

Elijah

THE NEXT FEW weeks fly by like a dream. Ember made the right choice in telling Everett the truth about us from the beginning. I'm glad I don't have to sneak around with her behind his back. She's not someone who should ever be kept a secret, and the guilt of lying to my best friend would have eaten me up inside. Every day I find out a new aspect of her personality that makes me fall deeper and deeper for her. Her rational way of thinking, her love of collecting houseplants in every room of our townhouse, her falling asleep with my arms wrapped around her every night. There's nothing about this woman that I don't love. The way she focuses so intently on each manuscript she reviews, like they're all the next great American novel, is probably one of her best qualities. Her belief in other people's dreams is astounding. She's so charismatic when she describes these stories to me, it's almost as if she wrote them herself. She asks me now and then if I'm interested in taking art classes in Charleston and I laugh. I don't think I've ever pictured myself in a classroom again, but it doesn't sound terrible.

Things have been quiet since Kelsea's last call and we've settled into a new routine. We all take turns making dinner, or in Everett's case, picking up takeout. Monday and Wednesday nights when Ev and I don't have clients, we all have what Ember has started calling 'family dinner.' Which is really just all of us gathered in the living room watching HGTV home remodeling shows. I'd love to say this was something Ember introduced us to, but it's not. Everett and I made a habit of HGTV marathons during our first tour overseas. We talked about how we would do things differently from the designers. It helped to take our minds off the shithole we were living in. What Ember doesn't know is why I'm so invested in these home renovation shows, but I plan on showing her today.

Last night I asked if she had time to take a trip with me today. She jumped at the chance, even though I know she's in the middle of reviewing at least three manuscripts. She seems to really be enjoying her job, which makes me so happy for her. I know what it's like to feel you're not living your dreams, so I'm glad she has that.

I'm leaning against the couch holding my extra

helmet, patiently waiting for my woman to make her way downstairs. Everett is in the kitchen stuffing his face with leftover Chinese from last night. "Dude, it's like 9am, that's nasty," I say, laughing at him.

"I give zero fucks. I'm starving and this is delicious. Don't hate me cuz' you ain't me, baby," he says, giving me a wink. He's such a fucking dumbass, but I'm glad to have his constant entertainment. "Hey, can I ask you something?" his tone suddenly sounding serious.

"Of course. What's on your mind?" I say, turning around to face him.

"This thing with you and my sister, is it for real? I mean, I know it's not my business. You guys are adults and whatever you do is up to you. But she's the most important person in my life, Elijah. I need to know she won't get her heart broken here." His concern is clearly etched across his face.

I knew this question would come, eventually. I'm not one for sharing my feelings, especially with another guy, but I feel like I owe it to him to be honest. "Honestly Ev, it's as real as it gets for me. It's still new and we're still figuring out how to be together. But I'm in this for the long-haul. I'm a better person with Ember in my life. She makes me want to be better. She makes me want things I've never even considered. All I can tell you is, if something happened to us, she wouldn't be the only one with a broken heart," I say, surprised at how much I just revealed to him and to myself.

I can see his smug grin as he nods his head. "Yeah, she has a way of bringing out the best in people, even if she doesn't see that. Our parents weren't very... supportive when we were growing up. They weren't negligent or anything, they just really didn't give a shit. Apathetic, I guess you could say. She used to say we were raising each other, and really she wasn't wrong. Just take care of her. She deserves someone who cares about her as much as she cares for them," he says, his love for his sister shining in his eyes.

"I'm gonna do my best, brother. I really care about her and I only want to see her happy. Hopefully she's happy with me," I tell him earnestly.

"She is. Twin telepathy, remember," he says, tapping a finger against his temple. "What do you have up your sleeve today?"

"I'm gonna show her the house," I say with a wide smile.

"No shit?!" He says, obviously shocked that I would bring her to my most private and personal place. I was honestly shocked with myself when the thought crossed my mind. I've never taken another woman there, never even considered it. But I want her to know every part of me. I don't want to have any secrets between us.

"Yeah, it just feels right. I feel like it's something she'll appreciate." My nerves are starting to get the best of me the longer she keeps me waiting.

"Well, good luck to you, man. I know she's gonna

love it," He says, slapping me on the shoulder and heading into his room.

I hear Ember's light footsteps coming down the stairs, and I turn to face her. No matter what, she always looks incredible. But today she's got on some hip-hugging black skinny jeans with rips down the legs and a tight grey t-shirt with her favorite red converse. She's braided her long blonde hair into a single thick braid that falls just a few inches above her perfect ass. Such a simple outfit, but on her it's sexy as fuck. I wanna peel those jeans down her legs and feast on her until she screams, but I'll save that for later. Right now, I've got other plans for her.

"Is this okay? I've never been on a motorcycle before, so I wasn't sure what to wear," she asks with a worried look on her face.

"Yeah, Sunshine, you look amazing. Just keep you legs away from the pipes and you'll be fine," I reach my hand out for hers. She laces her fingers with mine and we walk out to my bike. I can see the fear and hesitation written all over her face. "You know I'll keep you safe, right?" I ask.

"Of course, I'm just worried *I'm* gonna do something stupid and then we're gonna crash and die," she rambles on like she always does when she's nervous.

I place a quick kiss on her lips and drag her over to the side of my bike. "We're not gonna die, babe. That's a little dramatic. Climb on and swing your leg over to the other side. There are pegs right here for your feet," I say, showing her where to position herself. Once she's in place, I slide onto the seat in front of her, starting the engine. I hear a tiny squeal come from behind me and it's so damn adorable. "Scoot forward and wrap your arms around my waist," I tell her over the rumble of the engine. She slides forward until her front is flush with my back and I hear her let out a sigh as she wraps her arms around me, locking her hands in front of my waist. I place my hand on top of hers reassuringly and look back. "You ready?" I ask, and she gives me a shaky thumbs up, quickly locking her hands back in place. I laugh softly at her nervous excitement as I put it in gear and pull out onto the road.

sixteen

Ember

WE RIDE through town with the wind whipping around us. I cling to Eli's waist so tightly I'm surprised he can breathe. We pull to a stop at the last stoplight before the edge of town and I can feel Elijah's shoulders shaking as he laughs.

"I promise I won't let you fall off." He squeezes my hands and loosens my grip a little. "Just enjoy the ride, Sunshine." I take a second to survey the shops on Main Street. I haven't had much of a chance to explore yet, but I make a mental note to check out the eccentric-looking coffee shop on the corner with the bright yellow curtains. It looks like a great place to get out of the house when I need to edit. I could see myself making this place a home. I always thought I would end up in a big city surrounded by constant motion. But being in Grovewood makes me feel a kind of peace I've never felt before. I thought it might take a while for me to adjust to being here after campus life, but it was easy. It's like my mind has room to breathe here and I can finally center myself. The light turns green and Eli pats the side of my thigh, making sure I'm ready to ride. I lock my hands back around his waist and give him a small squeeze.

We drive a few miles out of town, passing rows of giant old oak trees draped with Spanish moss. This area is so beautiful surrounded by thick tree lines and marshes. The humidity is killer, but the view is so worth it. Just when I begin to wonder where the hell we're going, we turn down a dirt driveway with two enormous magnolia trees on each side. We drive down the winding driveway for almost a mile before pulling up in front of the most beautiful antebellum home I've ever seen. As soon as we park, I rip off my helmet, staring up at the house in awe.

"Oh my god, Elijah! This is incredible!" I'm practically screaming with excitement. Both levels have wide wrap-around porches with tall white pillars running from the foundation to the roof. Dark maroon shutters frame each of the eight windows on the front of the house, a stark comparison to the fresh white paint covering the rest of the structure. This is like something out of a dream. I've always read about homes like this and seen them in movies. Seeing the details up close is better than I ever could have imagined. I half imagine

Scarlet O'Hara to come strolling out the front door at any moment.

"You like it, Sunshine?" He asks, coming up behind me and wrapping his arms around my waist. I lean my head back against his chest, soaking in the warmth he provides.

"I love it. Do they give tours or something? I'd love to see the inside," I ask, taking a few steps closer.

"I could probably get you a tour, seeing as I own it," he replies, stopping me in my tracks. I turn around and face him, my eyes wide in surprise.

"What?! This is *yours*?!" I'm floored by his admission.

"Yeah, I bought it a few years ago and I've been bringing it back to life since then," he says casually.

I turn and instantly see the beautiful house with fresh eyes. Elijah did this. I try to imagine what it could have looked like when he first bought it. The wood on the front porch looks new, unmarred by age and time. I walk up the stairs to the front windows and peek inside.

"Can we go in? I'd love to see what you've done with the place," I say, beaming back at him.

"Yeah, the bottom floor is pretty much complete. The second floor still needs some work, but it's getting there." He pulls a set of keys from his pocket and unlocks the heavy oak front door, gesturing for me to step inside. If I thought the outside was amazing, it's nothing compared to what I see when he opens the door. He managed to incorporate modern details while still respecting the decades-old bones of the home. The entryway and parlor are massive and I can tell he kept the original wood floors, only restoring them to look new. I wander from room to room, in awe of the fact that he built this with his own hands. Even though the house has no furniture right now, I can imagine what each room would have looked like almost a hundred years ago. This is exactly what people are looking for when they talk about the South Carolina Low-Country.

"Well, what do you think?" he asks, startling me out of my imagination. He almost sounds nervous about what I'm gonna say next.

"What do I think? This is incredible, Elijah. You really restored all of this?" I run my hands over the dark brown bannister that leads upstairs, loving the feeling of the smooth wood under my hands.

"For the most part, yeah. I have a couple of buddies that came in to help with the plumbing and electrical work so I didn't burn the place down. Everett and I spent a few weekends repainting the entire exterior. But I stripped it down almost to the studs and rebuilt everything else. I still have a lot of work to do on the second level, but this floor is pretty much livable. The main bedroom is down here and the bathroom is fully functional. The kitchen is complete, minus some of the appliances," he gestures towards the back of the house.

"Oooooh! The kitchen!" I rush through the arched doorway and down the hall to find it. It's always my favorite part of all the home renovation shows we watch. I push open the doors and step into the kitchen of my dreams. I expected something a little more regal and a bit dated, but this kitchen is completely modern. The cabinets lining two walls are painted a cream color with dark brown trim. The tile backsplash is a dark forest green with a large farmhouse sink sunken into the countertop. It's a beautiful combination that reminds me so much of the forest that surrounds us. The few appliances already installed are stainless steel and pristine. He topped the large island stretching across the entire space with a gorgeous stained-wood butcher's block. I swear it's like he had a crystal ball to see into my mind. I wouldn't change a single thing about this kitchen.

"This is my favorite room in the entire house," I hear his deep timbre break the silence as he comes through the door and leans his elbows onto the bar.

"This is amazing. I swear you've been stealing ideas from my Pinterest board," I say jokingly, but he just shrugs. "Eli, *have* you been looking at my Pinterest board?" I ask, quirking my eyebrow in his direction.

"I don't even know what that is, Sunshine, but I do listen to you. I've made mental notes about things you've mentioned," he says, as if it's no big deal.

"Why would you do that?" I'm shocked that he would consider anything I said I would want in my future home.

"I'm not sure you get it, Ember. When I said I was all in, I meant it," he says softly but confidently, coming closer and placing his hands on my hips. "I never really saw a future that included anybody else until I met you. Now, when I think about what I want ten years from now, all I see is you," he says. I'm stunned by his admission. I knew I was falling so hard and so fast for this man, but I was sure he would think I was insane for feeling this much so soon. To hear him say he feels the same way causes warmth to wrap around my heart tightly and spread throughout my body.

I slowly wrap my arms around his neck, threading my fingers through his hair. His hands skate up and down the sides of my body until he slides them into my back pockets, pulling my body tightly against his. This is bliss. Being here in his arms, I feel safer than ever before. Like nothing and no one could ever touch me. Right here with this man is where I'm meant to be.

He bends down, pressing a soft kiss across my lips. This kiss is different from all the ones before. He's showing me exactly how he feels with this kiss. I pour every ounce of emotion I can into kissing him back. I'm hanging by a thread, trying not to get caught up and say something I know I can't take back. But with the feeling of his callused hands on my cheeks, his strong lips claiming mine, I feel all-consumed. Possessed and cherished so completely.

"I love you," I whisper, barely loud enough to be

heard. He instantly freezes, his lips still pressed to mine, motionless. I feel my body heating with unease, wondering if my confession is too much and way too soon. I try to pull away slightly, but he holds me firmly in place.

"Say it again," he says, pulling back just far enough to look at me. His blue eyes bore into mine. I take a deep breath and brace myself for whatever comes after this.

"I love you, Elijah," I say, never taking my gaze away from his. I want him to know I mean it and I'm not afraid. Even though deep down I'm terrified of his response.

Slowly, I see a smile creep over his face. He crashes his lips back down on mine, throwing his whole body into this kiss. "I love you too, Ember," he says between kisses and I feel the vice that has been squeezing my heart release. This man loves me.

I slide my arms around his neck as he picks me up, wrapping my legs around his waist. I can feel him walking to a different room, but I don't break this kiss. My need for oxygen can wait. The entire world can wait as long as I can keep kissing him. I feel him lean over and suddenly my back is pressed against something soft. I quickly open my eyes and realize we've moved into the master bedroom. He laid me down onto a massive king-sized platform bed, the cool silk sheets feeling like heaven against my heated skin. He kisses a path down my throat, his hand sliding under my shirt and across my stomach. My core clenches at the feeling of his rough hands on my skin and I let out a low moan. He growls in response and lifts himself up on his forearms, staring into my eyes. I can see the fire burning in his gaze and I know his control is hanging by a thread. He brushes a lock of my hair behind my ear, the love in his eyes palpable all around me.

"You gotta tell me where the boundaries are here, Em. I don't want to do anything you're not ready for." He searches my face for any sign of hesitation, but he won't find any.

"I don't want to have any boundaries with you, Eli," I say, pulling his shirt up and over his head. I run my fingers down his chiseled abs, stopping right above his belt buckle. His kisses become rougher and more urgent. He needs me just as badly as I need him, and I don't want to wait any longer. I give him a gentle push and sit up to take off my shirt and bra. He pushes me softly back down onto the sheets, peppering passionate kisses down my neck and slowly walking his fingers up my stomach until he covers my breast with his strong hand, kneading and teasing my nipple into a tight, almost painful bud. A shiver runs through my body and a heavy sigh escapes my lips. He covers my nipple with his mouth, nipping and sucking until I'm writhing beneath him.

"Please, Eli," I beg, "I need more." I buck my hips up, grinding my pelvis into his growing erection. He takes my nipple between his teeth and pulls gently. I moan loudly, not bothering to stay quiet. He swallows my moans, our lips clashing for control. My tongue darts out, swiping over his bottom lip. His hands are on the button of my jeans before I can catch my breath and I raise my hips up off the bed so he can get them off. The scrap of black lace covering my center is completely soaked through. I feel Eli tug sharply on one side of the strings until they snap. He tosses the scraps of fabric to the floor and slides his body down mine until his mouth is hovering over my core.

"You sure you're ready for this, baby?" He says, his lips barely touching me. "Because once I claim this sweet pussy, I don't think I'll ever give it back."

"God yes, Eli, please. Don't stop." I moan shamelessly.

His tongue swipes out, tasting me before diving in. He laps at me ferociously, sucking my clit into his mouth. My hips buck off the bed, my body already begging for release. He slides one thick finger between my folds, pumping in and out slowly at first, then faster and faster as I race closer to climax. When he stretches me with a second finger, I combust, screaming his name. His mouth covers my center as I come, causing my overly sensitized skin to tingle even more. I close my eyes, slowly coming down from the high as he kisses and licks his way back up my body until he meets my lips.

"I swear you could do that professionally," I laugh

but then reconsider as jealousy strikes through me at the thought of him with anyone else.

"Nobody but you, Sunshine." He says, reading my mind. I push him back onto the bed and move on top of him, straddling his hips and running my hand over the stubble growing on his face. He kisses my palm and the sweet gesture makes me smile. I kiss his chest over his heart softly, then make my way slowly down his abs, stopping at the sharp vee that stretches below his jeans. I unbutton his jeans and pull them down his legs, tossing them to the floor. The thick outline of his shaft is straining against the fabric of his boxer briefs. I peel them off of him and gasp, biting my lip at the sheer size of him.

"No fucking way," I say with a small squeal, "You're pierced?!" I'm not exactly shocked. Elijah Harding screams "bad boy". But I would have thought the man would have at least warned me. Not that I'm complaining. He lets out a deep chuckle at my surprise and I scoff, rolling my eyes.

"Don't tell me you've never seen a Prince Albert before," he gives me a wicked, sexy grin and the fire in my veins blazes hotter.

"Yeah, maybe in fantasy land where all the sexy as fuck men with pierced dicks live, babe, of course." I roll my eyes at his laughter and focus my attention back to where it belongs.

The drops of precum on the tip of his swollen head

tell me he's just as turned on as I am, and I'm more than willing to help him out with that. My tongue darts out to tease the ball at the tip of his piercing. He lets out a sharp hiss, and it's my turn to smirk. I wrap my lips around him, taking him as deep as I can before coming back up and doing it again. The muscles in his legs tighten and relax as he tries to keep his composure. I bob my head faster and faster, swirling my tongue around the tip, causing a deep growl to slip out of his throat. I feel him thread his fingers through my hair, controlling my pace, and I like him taking the reins. I want him to use my body in any way he needs to bring him pleasure. I trust him enough to let him. Suddenly, he pulls my head up, his thick shaft bobbing against his pelvis.

"Your mouth feels like heaven baby, but when I come it's gonna be deep in that sweet pussy," he says, quickly standing and walking over to his jeans. He pulls a condom out of his back pocket and tears it open with his teeth. I don't think I've ever seen anything sexier than this man rolling the condom down his length in such a hurry, knowing he can barely contain himself because of me.

I roll over on my back and spread my legs wide, putting myself on display for him. He stalks back to the bed, his eyes glued to my dripping wet center. He positions himself between my legs, rubbing the head of his dick over my clit. The curved barbell from his piercing causes a pressure and pleasure unlike anything I've ever known to flood my system and my back arches off the bed.

"Elijah, damn it! Stop fucking teasing me!" I yell, trying to pull my body closer to his. In one stroke, he plunges deep inside of me, filling me completely. My heart is pounding so loudly it blocks out all my other senses. Everything I feel, everything I see, it's all Elijah. He stays completely still for a few more moments as I adjust to his size. When he starts to move, sparks ignite throughout my entire body. The feeling of his skin sliding against mine, our bodies intertwined. It's incredible. I could spend my life wrapped up in this man and still never get enough.

"God, Ember, you're so fucking tight," he says, sweat dripping down his body and onto mine. I hold on tight to his shoulders as his strokes become harder and faster. I can see the tension building in his body, and I know he's getting close. He slides one hand down between us to stroke my clit and I cry out, the pleasure overwhelming me. I never knew sex could feel this way. Then again, I've never had sex with anyone I truly loved. Or anyone who really knew what they were doing, apparently. Elijah rubs my clit in tight circles, bringing me closer and closer to the edge. I arch my back off the bed, meeting him thrust for thrust. "Come for me, baby," he says, hiking my leg up over his hip to giving him a deeper angle. That's all it takes for me to fall apart, my walls squeezing and pulsing around him tightly.

"Oh fuck, Elijah, don't stop," I moan, clinging to his body. I know my nails are leaving marks all over his chest and arms, but I don't care. I've barely recovered from my last orgasm before I feel the next one building. His pace becomes frantic as he pulls my other leg up to my chest. I feel his cock swell inside me, and I know he won't last much longer. He reaches a hand up and tweaks my nipple, pinching the peak between his fingers. The sensation combined with his punishing thrusts is enough to send me back over the edge. He thrusts deeply once more and holds himself there, grunting as he empties himself into the condom.

He supports his weight over me for a few moments as we both catch our breath. He falls on top of the bed next to me, pulling my body close to him and draping his arm over my stomach. He rubs lazy circles across my skin on my stomach as we both come down from the adrenaline.

"Holy fuck. That was incredible," he says, his breathing still coming in pants. He gives me a sweet kiss on the forehead and rolls out of bed, walking to the bathroom to dispose of the condom. I hear the water turn on and I will my body to get up, but I have no energy left. Suddenly, I feel him kneel on the bed between my legs and place a warm washcloth over my sensitive core. He slowly drags the cloth over my skin, cleaning me up, and my heart fills even more than I thought possible. I've never had another person touch me so intimately, so lovingly. I feel the tears well up in my eyes and I will them away. I won't be that girl that cries after the most incredible sex of her life. He places a soft kiss on my inner thigh and tosses the washcloth to the floor.

"Well," I say, breaking the silence, "I think I might like this room even more than the kitchen." His riotous laugh is music to my ears, and he pulls me closer to his side.

"You're only saying that because you haven't seen the master bathroom yet," he says, and I realize he's right. We cut our tour short and I'm not even a little bit sorry.

"Alright then, tour guide," I say, rolling out of his reach and pulling his t-shirt over my head, "show me the rest."

seventeen

Elijah

RIDING BACK HOME with Ember pressed tightly to my back is like heaven. Something shifted back at the plantation, as if this became something so much more from the second we walked through those doors. I knew then that I could see myself making that place a home with her. The moment she said she loved me, I knew I had to make her mine in a forever kind of way.

I've done my best these last few weeks to keep her mind off the nightmare she ran from in Durham, but I know it's still haunting her. She thinks no one sees her double check when she locks the door or the way she's always looking over her shoulder any time we leave the house, but I see it. I hate that this asshole has made her live in fear. I wish I could take her pain away, but I know the best I can do is keep her safe.

We pull up to the house and head inside through the

garage door. I could have sworn I'd locked it behind me when we left, but maybe I hadn't. As I turn the doorknob, it feels loose in my hand. I make a mental note to fix that tonight. The last thing we need right now is lax security.

Everett stands in the kitchen, watching baseball and eating cereal at four in the afternoon. Sometimes I swear he's twelve years old. "Hey guys, you have fun?" he asks without looking away from the game.

"Yeah, it was amazing," Ember says with a huge smile. I'm surprised at how happy it makes me to know I'm the one who put that smile on her face.

"That house is so fucking badass. I think you'll have to make room for me there too, Eli," he mumbles as he shovels another spoonful of Cocoa Puffs into his mouth. "You got a package delivered while you were out, Sparky" he points to the long rectangular box lying on the corner of the bar. Out of the corner of my eye, I see Ember move towards the box, then stop dead in her tracks. I look over at her and all the color has drained from her face. Her hands are shaking by her sides and the fear in her eyes is palpable from across the room.

"What's wrong, Ember?" I come to her side instantly. Everett looks over at us, concern on his face.

"That... that box... I got a box just like it before I left Duke... from Justin." She says the last part so quietly it's barely a whisper. I feel rage building throughout my body.

"Everett, open it," I say, wrapping my arms tightly around Ember and pulling her into my chest. Her hands clutch tightly into my shirt. I can feel her body trembling as I rub my hands up and down her back. "It's ok, Sunshine. It's gonna be okay," I tell her as calmly as I can. Everett pulls open the lid and I can see the tips of crimson red roses poking out of the top. He picks up a card from inside, reads it, and throws the box against the wall.

"FUCK! This guy is a fucking psycho," he screams, his breaths coming in heavy pants. His fists are clenched tightly at his sides and the look in his eyes is murderous.

"What does it say, Ev?" she says, her face still buried in my chest.

"Are you sure you even wanna know, Em?" I ask.

"Yes. I obviously can't hide. I have to know what it says." She looks up at me with fear and uncertainty in her eyes.

Everett hands her the card and bends down to clean up the mess he made with the flowers. She takes a small step back, but I don't let her go. Turning the card over in her hand, she reads it out loud,

Ember

This cat-and-mouse game you're playing has been fun. I do appreciate your attempt at keeping things interesting. But you should know by now that I'll always find you, no matter

where you hide. Don't worry my dear, I'll forgive your indiscretion with that tattooed degenerate. Everyone needs to sow their wild oats before they settle down. As long as you behave yourself from here on out, I won't have to punish you. I'll be watching.

Justin

She crumples the paper up in her hand and throws it to the ground. Tears are rolling down her face and she doesn't hide them. I look to the floor where the remains of the bouquet lies and I see a photo lying there. I pick it up and study it, already knowing I remember exactly when this was taken. I took Ember to the bookshop in town two weeks ago to browse and we ended up in the back row of romance novels. The picture shows us locked in a passionate kiss with Ember's back pushed up against the bookshelf as I cup her ass. I remember it vividly and I feel rage burning inside of me. Knowing that intimate moment between the two of us was tainted by him makes me furious.

"God damnit!" She screams, "How did he find me here? How did he even know where I am? What did I do to deserve this?" She asks, more to herself than anything else.

"Nothing, Ember." I reach out to pull her back into my arms. "You didn't ask for any of this. He's obviously a fucking crazy son of a bitch. This isn't on your shoulders," I kissing the top of her head, trying to soothe the pain and fury coming off her in waves.

I look over at Everett while she sobs heavily against my chest. He's barely keeping his anger under control, and I know the feeling. I see him jerk his head towards the back door and I give him a small nod.

"Why don't you go take a long shower and calm down? Ev and I will clean up this shit and take care of dinner. You can rest for a while," I say, softly kissing her forehead. She sniffles and nods her head, no fight left in her eyes. It kills me to see her look so defeated. She shuffles upstairs and I watch her walk into my room and shut the door.

I gather up the flower box, card, and picture, and walk out the back door with Everett trailing behind me. I throw the box into the trashcan on the deck, tossing the card and picture on the patio table.

"What the fuck do we do here, Elijah?" He asks, lighting a cigarette and falling into one of the deck chairs.

"I honestly don't know, man," I drag my hand down my face roughly.

"I mean, this is some seriously psycho shit. I feel like we need to take this to the cops," he says.

"I agree with you there, but I can already see how that's gonna go. They're gonna tell her she has no proof that it was him and there's nothing they can do until he actually harms her," I say, leaning against the railing.

"So we're just supposed to fucking sit around and wait for him to hurt her?! No fucking way! I won't do that, Eli! I can't believe you would just let this go," he shouts, obviously close to losing his shit.

"That's not what I said, Ev. I'd never let him touch her. He'd fucking die before he even got close," I say fiercely. "We just need to make a plan here."

"Oh, I have a plan. Find this fucker and put him in the ground," he says viciously.

"A plan that doesn't end with you and I both in jail would be nice," I tell him, trying to remain reasonable.

"Fine. I know she's gonna be pissed, but I don't think she should go out by herself anymore. Apparently, he knows exactly where she is and we can't keep her locked up in here like a fucking prisoner." He sounds emotionally exhausted and I know the feeling.

"I agree. I know she won't like it, but I think it's what we have to do. I'll call tomorrow morning and see about getting a better alarm system put in here, just in case. Until we figure out where the hell this guy is, she can come to the shop with us when we're both working. She can pretty much work from anywhere, so the only thing it's gonna hurt is her pride." I say, knowing she's probably gonna raise hell about having to be babysat. Usually, I like the fire in her personality. But this time I can't give in to her. I won't. Her safety is more important than anything else.

"Yeah, good luck to your balls when you tell her that

news," Everett says, laughing at my pained expression, "I would say I'll tell her, but I know how much she *loves* being told what to do so that's all you, dude."

"Thanks so much for the vote of confidence, Ev. Your support is so encouraging," I say as sarcastically as I possibly can. I take a deep breath and head back inside. I climb the stairs slowly, bracing myself for what's to come when I find my woman.

eighteen

Ember

I'M STANDING under the shower head, letting the scorching hot water run over my body. I don't care about the pain it's causing. It's nothing compared to the ache in my chest I feel right now. Today started out as an incredible day. Elijah sharing his home with me and everything that happened after that was better than anything I could have imagined. But yet again, Justin has taken something beautiful in my life and twisted it until it's become a living nightmare. He's been watching me with Eli. How did he even find me in Grovewood? This town is barely on the map. I make a mental note to call Kelsea after this and ask her if she knows anything.

On the plus side, seeing the fiercely protective side of Elijah is something I could get used to. I've never been the 'damsel in distress' type. I've always been more of a Jo March or Katniss Everdeen, save my own damn self, independent type of woman. Sure, my brother has always been ridiculously overprotective, but we've been apart for so many years that I've learned to depend more on myself. Honestly, I enjoy being this way. It's wonderful to have a big, strong, sexy man like Elijah willing to protect you at all costs, but it's so much more valuable to be able to do it yourself.

I hear the bathroom door open and close. I can tell Eli is in the room even though he doesn't make a move to disturb me. "Talk. I'm sure you and my brother have formed some kind of plan for what *you* think is best for *my* life," I say, emphasizing the last part.

"It's not like that, Ember. We just want to protect you," he says, his voice strained with worry. I hate to hear him so distressed. I know he and Everett have the best of intentions. It just rubs me the wrong way that neither one of them asked my opinion on the matter. Sure, I cried after I read the note Justin left. But I got my shit together pretty quickly. I'm not some simpering little girl who can just be carried around like a rag-doll.

"I understand that, Elijah. Do I get a say at all in any of this? Or am I just supposed to nod my head and smile about whatever you both decide?" I know my voice sounds a little more bitter than I intended, but I can't help it.

"How about we make a deal, sugar? I'll tell you the plan we've come up with, and once I'm done explaining why we think it's for the best, then you can change any part of it you want as long as you can tell me why," he bargains with me, still keeping his distance behind the shower curtain.

I lean my back against the shower tile, crossing my arms. "Go ahead. Give me your plan." I roll my eyes behind the curtain because he can't see me, anyway.

"I'm gonna call tomorrow morning and see about getting a better alarm system put in here, something that monitors all the doors and windows that we can access remotely," he says.

"Ok, that sounds reasonable. But I'm paying for half of whatever you decide to put in." I force strength into my voice and hope he won't argue. I hear him grumble, but he doesn't object, at least not out loud. "Go on," I say, considering his silence a win.

"We have no idea where this asshole is, Ember. He could be all the way back in Durham, or he could be right down the street. I have a buddy who has a knack for tracking people down. I'm gonna reach out to him tonight and see what he can find out. Until we figure out where the hell he is, Everett and I would both feel more at ease if you came to the shop with us when we're both working. I know it sounds like a big ask, and I know how much you value your independence. But I don't know how I'm gonna be able to focus on anything at work if I know you're here alone, babe." I know he's playing on my emotions by telling me it would make him and Everett more comfortable, but a part of me also knows they're right. If I'm honest, I'm not sure I want to be alone here, anyway.

"Okay, I think I could do that," I mumble. The shower curtain slides opens abruptly and I'm staring into Elijah's piercing blue eyes.

"You're really not gonna put up a fight here?" He asks, obviously surprised by my quick acceptance.

"I'm not gonna say I like the idea of having babysitters all the time," I say, placing my hand on my hip, "but I know it's the best choice. Strength in numbers and all that. Besides, I'm not super fond of the idea of being here by myself if both of you have to be at the shop," I reply, shrugging my shoulders.

Before I know it, Elijah is stepping into the shower, fully clothed. He wraps his arms around me tightly, the tension in his shoulders releasing slightly.

"Honey, you do realize you're still fully clothed, right?" I ask with a grin.

"Yep," he says, not lifting his head from the crook of my neck for even a second. He takes a deep breath, seeming to center himself as he holds me tighter.

"And you realize you're probably gonna ruin your boots, right?" I ask.

"Don't care," he replies. I wrap my arms around his waist and rub my hands down his soaking wet shirt. I'm filled with gratitude that this man cares for me so much that he is this relieved to know I won't fight him about my safety.

"If you wanted to join me, you just had to ask," I say seductively, trying to ease his tension even more. He hesitates a moment longer before pulling away from me. I almost think he's gonna leave me here, wet and wanting. He steps out of the shower and kicks his boots off by the door. He strips his soaking wet t-shirt over his head, revealing the delicious tattoos of branches and vines that run from the top of his hands, up his forearms, across his collarbone, and finally snake down his torso. They disappear right below his belt, and I always want to follow their path. He is a seriously beautiful man. I'd love nothing more than to run my tongue over every inch of those tattoos. He quickly strips out of his jeans and boxers before stepping into the shower behind me. I wrap my arms around his neck and lay my head against his chest. His arms encircle my waist, squeezing me tightly before placing a kiss on my wet hair.

"I love you, Ember. I promise I'll protect you. He's never going to touch you again," he says with a conviction I have no choice but to believe.

"I know you will, Eli. I love you, too," I say, reaching up and pulling his lips down to mine.

nineteen

Ember

I MANAGED to make the best out of being stuck at the shop late at night with the guys. They brought in a comfy oversized chair for the lobby, a truly heartfelt gesture from two tough tattooed biker guys. I lounge there reading and editing until one of them is ready to go. Tonight they both have late clients so we won't get out of here until well past 1am, but I don't mind. Clients tell me their stories behind the tattoos they want and I enjoy listening to them. I've even tried to learn the basics of their digital scheduling system so their receptionist, Willow, can take a night off occasionally. I've learned that she's a single mom, so I'm more than happy to give her a break. I don't mind pitching in here. It keeps my mind off wondering where Justin could be.

I hear the bell above the door ring and I pull my eyes from the steamy romance I'm editing to watch a tall, tan, and beautiful girl walk through the door. Her long chocolate brown hair is braided into two French pigtails down her back, but she makes it look badass. The sleeve of wildflower tattoos that cover her left arm looks so vivid I could almost pick them right off her skin. She glances around the lobby as if she's looking for someone specific.

"Is there somebody I can help you find?" I ask her. "Did you have an appointment tonight?"

"No, I'm just dropping in, but I'm sure Eli will be able to fit me in," she says with a cocky smirk on her face.

The way she says Eli's name, like it's so familiar to her, has me instantly on edge. Over the past week I've spent camping in the lobby, I've seen every female client who comes through the door shoot their shot with my man. But I've also seen him brush them all off, making sure he kisses me before he goes back to work every time. I take a calming breath and regain my composure.

"Well, I think his schedule is full tonight, but I can ask if he can fit you in," I say, forcing some cheerfulness into my voice. I would never want to affect his reputation or business just because I feel a little jealousy. "I'll just go ask him. Be right back." I drop my work onto my comfy chair with a loud plop and walking back to Eli's room.

He looks up from the dagger he's working on for another local vet and gives me that beautiful smile of his. "Hey babe, to what do I owe the pleasure of seeing your gorgeous face?" he asks and I roll my eyes, laughing at his cheesy flattery. He really lays it on thick sometimes.

"Well, there's a girl here for you," I say, looking back towards the counter. The girl seems to be examining the artwork on each wall incredibly closely. "Seems like she knows you. She said she was sure you could fit her in tonight." I try to keep my expression neutral, but I'm sure he sees right through me.

"What girl? This is my only client tonight," he says, gesturing to the man sitting in the chair next to him. "Did she give a name?" He asks, looking confused.

"No, no name. Just said she was here for you," I say, trying my best not to sound catty and annoyed.

"Ok, give me just a sec and I'll be right out to deal with her," he says, finishing the shading on the dagger's tip.

I walk back to the lobby and find the girl staring intently at the picture of my brother and Eli when they were deployed. They both drop vague comments now and then about that time, but I don't pry. In this picture, they're standing next to a camel and Everett looks like he's trying to hump its leg. My brother, ladies and gentlemen. So classy.

"He said he'll be right out. He's finishing up an appointment now," I tell her.

"Ok, no problem, I've got nothing but time," she says

with a beautiful smile. Something about her smile is so familiar, but I just can't place it.

I drop back into my chair and pick up the manuscript. I had forgotten I was in the middle of reading an incredibly well-detailed sex scene and now it seems inappropriate since I'm no longer alone. I look over at her and find her staring at me intently. My cheeks heat under her attention. "Something wrong?" I ask.

"What are you reading?" She replies, ignoring my question entirely.

"Umm, it's a manuscript from an author who's trying to get published by the company I work for," I say, giving her as few details as possible.

"Must be some manuscript if it's got you blushing like that," she says, gesturing in my direction. Damn my mother for giving me such fair skin.

"Oh god," I say, burying my face in my hands, "Sorry, it's a pretty spicy romance." I try to laugh off my embarrassment.

"Oooooh, my favorite kind!" She says, clapping her hands excitedly. I smile at her reaction. Most people think romance novels are smut or trashy, but some of the strongest females I've ever met have been characters in romance novels.

"Yeah, I really enjoy reading this genre the most," I tell her, raising my eyebrows, "plus it gives me plenty of new ideas to use on my boyfriend," I say and we both bust out laughing.

"Rory?" I hear the deep timbre of Eli's voice and turn my head to see him walking our way.

"Elijah!" she screams and runs to him. He immediately wraps her in a hug, picking her up off the ground and spinning her around. She kisses his cheek and hugs him back tightly.

"What the hell are you doing here? Why didn't you tell me you were coming?" He says sternly, placing her back on her feet.

"I don't need your permission, Elijah. Besides, I thought you said I was always welcome," she says, crossing her arms and cocking her hip to one side.

"Of course, you're always welcome. I just like to have a heads up in case something happens on the way," he says. I sit quietly, watching the conversation volley back and forth between the two of them.

I clear my throat and gather my stuff. "I'm just gonna go back into the kitchen and give you guys some privacy," I stand and pick up my scattered notes.

"Shit! My bad, babe. This is my baby sister, Aurora. Aurora, this is Ember," he says, gesturing back and forth between us.

"Oh my gosh! You're Ember?!" she says, excitedly. It warms my heart to know he's told her about me. I knew his sister and mom were still back in his hometown in Louisiana, but I didn't know much else about them. The jealousy I felt moments before instantly melts away, replaced with nervous energy.

"Yeah, that's me," I say, giving her a small wave. "It's so nice to finally meet you." She quickly pulls me in for a huge hug which stuns me momentarily, but eventually I return it.

"Sorry," she says, shrugging, "I'm a hugger. You can call me Rory, everyone does. I've heard so much about you. I was hoping you would be as awesome as Elijah told me you were, luckily it seems like you are." At this point, I'm sure I'm as red as a tomato.

"Oh, thank you so much," I say awkwardly. "Seeing you two together, I can't believe I didn't notice the resemblance as soon as you walked through the door." Aurora has the same dark brown hair and crystal blue eyes I see every day on Elijah. Standing next to each other, it's incredibly obvious they're related.

"Okay, okay, what are you doing here, Bug? Is everything okay with mom?" he asks, concern etched across his face.

"Oh yeah, mom's fine. I just needed to get away for a little while. Erik and I broke up again and I'm done for good this time. I just didn't want to be there when he comes to grovel," she says, looking down at her shoes. I know all about running from ex-boyfriends, so I don't blame her for running straight to her big brother. I did the same thing.

"Do I need to kick his ass? You know I already hate that asshole. I'd gladly do it," Eli says.

"No, bubba. I just needed to clear my head, and I thought the crisp South Carolina air would be just what I needed." She gives him a small, weak smile.

He steps closer to her, wrapping her in a hug. "Of course it's what you needed. You're welcome to stay as long as you need to." He tells her. Their tenderness towards each other is so heart-warming. "Let me wrap things up and clean up my station, then we can all head home," he says, nodding to us both. He drops a quick kiss on my forehead and walks back to his room.

"That's so fucking adorable," Rory says, with a huge grin on her face as she watches us.

"Oh, I totally agree," I say, smiling back at her.

twenty

Elijah

I'M ALWAYS happy to see my sister. I think it's been almost a year now since I've hugged her. But having her show up in the middle of this shit-storm with Ember's ex is just horrible timing. Still, when she told me the reason for her making the trip, there was no way I could turn her away. I've always thought her on-again off-again boyfriend, Erik, was a piece of shit. But that mostly has to do with the fact that every time she tells me anything about him, it's bad.

Pulling into the driveway, I park my bike close to the garage door to give Rory room to park her Bronco. Why she's kept that truck all these years, I have no clue. It gets shit gas mileage and there's always something broken on it, but it's her baby, so she just keeps fixing it up. I hold my hand out, helping Ember climb off behind me, and she unlocks the side door to the house.

"Who's hungry?" Rory says the second she walks through the door.

"Only you, Bug. I told you we could have stopped for food on the way home and you said no." That girl has always had an appetite bigger than mine. She walks over to the fridge and opens the door wide.

"Holy shit! There's actual food in here!" She says, faking shock. I roll my eyes at her sarcasm.

"Ha-ha, real funny. There's been food in there every time you've been here," I say.

"Yeah, leftover Chinese and hot pockets. Real gourmet shit there, bubba," she says and I hear Ember suppressing a laugh beside me. "I like this girl, bro. She's an excellent influence on your eating habits."

"You say that, but you didn't watch her eat 2 pop tarts and half a Snickers bar for breakfast," Ember smacks my shoulder for revealing her secrets, which only makes me laugh harder.

"Rude," Ember says with a grin, "it was only 1 pop tart." The way she fits so seamlessly into my life is amazing. Seeing her here with my sister, smiling and talking with her like they are old friends, it makes me so damn happy.

Rory grabs a bag of chips and falls down onto the couch. "Anybody got an extra blanket?" She asks.

"What? No. You don't need to sleep on the couch," Ember says beside me.

"Well, there are mosquitos outside and I'm not

kicking you out of your bed, so I'm cool with couch surfing," Rory replies.

"It's ok, Bug. Ember can sleep with me. She already does pretty much every night anyway," I say without thinking, eliciting a smile from Ember's face that warms me all the way to my core. As soon as I extend the invitation, I want to take it back, but it's too late. I don't sleep with anyone for their safety and mine, so I'm not sure why I even suggested that.

"Yeah, it's totally fine. I just washed the sheets and everything, so it's all clean." Ember says, leaving Rory no room to argue.

"I guess as long as you haven't been banging my brother in that bed, then I'll take it," Rory replies and Ember turns ten shades of red as she silently walks upstairs. Rory and I both watch her from the living room as she grabs her pajamas and heads into my room.

"I like her, bubba. She seems like she's really good for you," Rory says, smiling up at me.

I put my arm around her and pull her in for a side hug. "Yeah, I agree. She's really incredible, not sure why she picked me," I laugh.

"Because you're pretty incredible too, big brother," she says, standing on her tiptoes and kissing my cheek. She heads up the stairs in front of me, turning into Ember's room.

"By the way, the bathroom is out of commission in there, so you'll have to use mine or Everett's," I say, noticing the shiver of disgust when I mention Everett's bathroom.

"Ok, no problem," she says, turning around and closing the door.

I walk into my room and see Ember standing in the bathroom, brushing her teeth. She's wearing my t-shirt and a pair of boy short underwear that makes her ass look delectable. I lean against the door frame, just enjoying the view. We lock eyes in the mirror and she grins. This woman will be the death of me, I swear. Not only is she so beautiful and strong, she's also incredibly fucking sexy, a temptress without even trying. I don't think she even realizes how many men watch her every time we go out.

"You should take a picture. It'll last longer," she says, pulling me from my thoughts.

"If I thought you wouldn't kill me for it, I just might," I say with a smirk.

"Not gonna happen, honey. You'll just have to commit me to memory," she says, smiling and coming over to wrap her arms around my neck. She threads her fingers through the long hair at the nape of my neck and I love that feeling. It's something I've come to expect from her every time she's in my arms and it's just so exclusively Ember. Just having her near me, touching me, is instantly relaxing.

"I couldn't forget you if I tried, Sunshine," I bend down, stealing slow kisses as we back up to the bed. "I guess I kinda sprang this whole 'sharing a room' thing on you. I should probably tell you that I'm not the most sound sleeper. Sometimes I have nightmares. It's not something I'm happy about and I've been working on it, but it is what it is. I don't wan't to hurt you or scare you. Are you sure okay with this?" I ask.

"Spend all night lying next to my hot boyfriend or spend all night alone on the couch with my poptarts? How ever will I choose?" she rolls her eyes and I laugh as I strip out of my jeans and pull her down onto the bed next to me. We lay tangled together in silence for several long minutes before she speaks, "I'll be okay. A nightmare next to you is better than a daydream anywhere else," she grins at me, and I'm so in awe of her. I don't know how she remains so optimistic, even with everything going on around us. We could be standing in the middle of a hurricane, but according to her, as long as we're together then the storms don't matter.

"I really like your sister," she whispers.

"Yeah, she's great. She really likes you, too. She's always hoping somebody will 'tame my wild ways' as she calls it," I tell her.

"Is that what I'm doing? Taming you?" She asks with apprehension in her voice.

"I think you're saving me, Ember," I tell her with conviction. "Without you, I don't think I would have ever considered building a future with anyone. For the first time, it seems worth it."

She sits up next to me, looking over my features to see the honesty in what I've just told her. She crashes her lips to mine, surprising me. I kiss her back with the same passion she's pouring into me. She sits up to pull her shirt over her head, momentarily breaking our connection. I seize my chance to give each of her nipples the attention they deserve. She moans softly as she pulls my head tighter against her chest. I nip and suck her perfect pink buds until she's writhing on the sheets under me. In one swift motion, I roll her over so she's lying on top of me. I pull her lips down to mine, craving the taste of them. Sliding my tongue into her mouth, I savor the sweet cinnamon taste of my girl. She sits up to catch her breath, rubbing her pussy against the growing ridge of my dick. I pull her hips tighter against mine and her eyes snap open, desire quickly overcoming her control. She lifts up long enough to slide her panties off her legs and falls back down, grinding on my aching cock. I shove my boxers down and I can feel how wet she is as she slides easily over me. "Condom, babe," I say tightly as she kisses down my jaw, my control barely hanging on.

She stops suddenly, sitting up and looking directly into my eyes. "I'm clean. I got tested after Justin and I haven't been with anyone since. You?"

"Yeah, I'm clean. Just had a physical a few weeks back and you're the only one I've been with since." I reply, rubbing my thumb in circles across her hip bones.

She lifts up, positioning my cock at her entrance. Slowly, she slides back down until she's taken every inch of me inside of her. She feels so amazing at this angle. Knowing there's nothing separating us makes me feel a sense of trust and love that I've never felt with anyone before now. She looks like a goddess, her golden hair falling around her shoulders like curtains of sunlight, slowly riding me and letting little moans escape her lips each time she comes down.

"Oh, god Elijah, you feel so..." her words trail off as her speed picks up. I can see the pleasure build in her, her legs quivering and her breaths coming in short pants. She is so close to the edge. I slide my hand down between us and rub her clit in fast circles. I feel the exact moment when she shatters, her walls clenching around me like a vise. I thrust up into her faster and harder, chasing my own release. She meets me thrust for thrust, circling her hips as she comes down. As soon as I feel her tightening around my shaft again, I know I'll follow her over the edge this time. I grasp her hips and pull her down against me, causing my pelvic bone to grind into her clit. She screams, her pussy squeezing me so tightly I can't hold on any longer. My cock thickens, exploding inside of her, claiming her in a way I've never claimed another woman before.

I hold her tightly to my body, our breathing labored and our skin covered in a sheen of sweat. We lie in comfortable silence until an alarming thought pops into my head.

"Uh, babe, are you on the pill?" I ask and feel her shoulders shake as she laughs.

"Now you ask that?" She says, looking up at me with her eyebrows raised. I guess it is a little late to think about protection now.

"Well, I was kinda distracted before, so it slipped my mind," I tell her, smacking her ass lightly. She giggles and burrows closer into my chest.

"Yes, honey, I'm not fantastic at remembering to take it, so I'll have to work on that. But I'm covered. I wouldn't have kept going if I wasn't. I'm not the baby trapping kind," she says.

"That's good, because I totally am and at least one of us should be responsible here," I joke, and she looks at me like I've lost my mind. I laugh, loudly and wholeheartedly. She rolls her eyes and lays her head back down. I don't remember a time when I've ever felt this peaceful.

twenty-one

Ember

OVER THE NEXT FEW DAYS, we fall into a comfortable routine. You would think the house might be crowded with four people and three bedrooms, but it's not. Aurora and I discovered we enjoy a lot of the same things, so we've been sharing books and watching reality TV together. I can see her becoming a great friend. Sharing a room with Elijah has been better than I imagined. I was a little apprehensive after he told me about his nightmares, but so far he's kept them under control. Sometimes he thrashes in his sleep or releases these pained moans, and I know he's trapped in the memories of his past. During those moments, I try to stroke his back softly or whisper calming reassurance until he settles. When the dreams are particularly vivid enough to wake him from his sleep, I allow him to find his solace in my body until we're both too exhausted to move. At first, I was afraid he would say I snore or something totally embarrassing, but I just feel like that's where I belong.

Eli has been talking back and forth with some guy he calls Breaker about tracking down Justin. I guess he's pretty tech savvy and can hack into a bunch of places that sound semi-illegal, so I'm not asking questions. I've thrown most of my time and energy into my work and tried to block out anything related to Justin. Unfortunately, I still feel like I need to look over my shoulder every time I leave the house. I want to feel safe in this town, but I can't shake the feeling of unease.

Today, for the first time in a while, Eli and Everett agreed Rory and I would be safe to go out without them as long as we stayed together. I'm excited to check out the bookstore in town again and Rory wants to find some new clothes. Once we're dressed and ready to go, we hop in the Jeep and head into town.

"I think you're really great for my brother," Rory says, climbing out of my Jeep in front of Revamp, the cute vintage clothing store in the middle of town.

"I think he's pretty fantastic for me, too." I smile at her compliment, adoring the fact that other people can see our love for each other.

"He's never been one to do much for his own benefit," she says, holding open the door as we walk inside. "He's always done what he could to take care of me and my mom, even though it wasn't his responsibility."

"That sounds like Eli," I say with a smile. "I didn't ask him to change his life for me and all the drama that surrounds me. He just did it."

"That's because he loves you, Ember. I'm glad he found someone who is worthy of him," she says, grinning.

"I wish he didn't have to deal with all this bullshit from my ex, but I'm not willing to give him up. So, I guess me and my drama are a package deal," I say with a shrug.

Rory laughs with a mischievous gleam in her eyes, "That's okay, keeps him on his toes," she winks back at me.

We browse through rows and rows of vintage band shirts, trying on styles from different eras and enjoying some much-needed girl time. Before we know it, it's been three hours and we're finally hauling our bags to the Jeep.

"Oh my god, Ember! What the hell happened?!" Rory screams beside me, dropping her bags as she covers her mouth with her hands in shock.

I look over to my Jeep and see that all four tires are flat and the word 'WHORE' has been keyed into the passenger door. I feel the sting of tears welling up in my eyes and I let them fall silently. "Why? How? Why is this happening?" I ask, barely above a whisper. I can hear Rory already talking on the phone with someone, most likely Elijah.

"Yeah, come now. We're on Main and Maplewood at Revamp. It's really terrible, Eli," she says, "Ok, I'll call the police now, see you in a minute." She hangs up and walks us slowly over to a bench in front of the store, sitting me down and piling our bags next to me. I'm stunned. I can't speak, can't move. He was right here, close enough to touch me, and I didn't even know. The thought of something horrible happening to me, or worse to Rory, makes my stomach turn. I pull my knees up under my chin and sit quietly on the bench like a frightened child. Why me? I hear the familiar rumble of Elijah's motorcycle drawing closer, but I'm frozen. From the corner of my eye, I see him stop quickly at the curb and hug Rory, making sure she's okay. Then he's kneeling in front of me. His electric blue eyes lock onto mine and I break. I launch myself into the safety of his arms and release the sobs I've been holding back. He wraps his arms around me tightly, supporting my weight and running his hand down my back soothingly.

"It's okay, Sunshine. I'm here. I'm right here," he says, his tone calm and comforting.

"He was here, Elijah! Right here, and I didn't even notice! He could have seriously hurt Aurora or done something just as insane and I didn't even fucking notice!" I'm screaming at this point, but I don't care. The fear and rage I've been trying to keep under control courses through my body freely. "How can he do this? How is there nothing we can do but wait around for him to do something even more dangerous?" my eyes plead for answers, but I know he has none.

"We can do something now, baby. Veiled threats and creepy notes are one thing, but this is serious property damage. We're gonna tell the police everything we know, and then they'll pick him up. He won't get away with it this time," the anger is tangible in his voice.

A patrol car pulls up behind Elijah's bike and two officers step out. Over the next hour, we explain to them everything we know and give them as much information as possible. They take pictures of my Jeep and tell us they will check with the local shops to see if anyone has a security video that could have caught something.

"It would be nice if you still had one of those notes," the older, more seasoned officer says.

"Actually, I do," Elijah says, and I look at him in confusion.

"You do?" I say, remembering him telling me he got rid of the last box Justin sent.

"Yeah, I threw away the flowers and shit, but I kept the card, just in case. I was afraid something like this would happen and we might need it," he says, rubbing his hand over the back of his neck.

"Well, if you could bring that by the station, that would be great. We'll look into this lead and keep in touch with any new developments," the officer says, shaking Elijah's hand and walking back to his car.

"I'm glad you kept that," I whisper.

"What can I do here, Ember? I want to help you feel better, but I don't know how." He sounds so lost and I'm right there with him.

I place my hand against his cheek and pull his lips down to mine, giving him a tender kiss. "I love you for wanting to help me, honey. Just take me home." I suddenly feel exhausted from the adrenaline crash.

"Rory, you feel okay to take the Jeep over to the repair shop with the tow guy? It's about four blocks that way and Everett said he can meet you there and bring you back home," he says. I see her nod her head quietly and I instantly feel guilt for her sadness and fear. If I hadn't run here, these things wouldn't be affecting these people who I've come to love so much.

"Come on, Em," Eli says, grabbing my hand and pulling me over to the curb where his bike is parked. "You feel okay to ride?" He asks, softly rubbing my cheek with his thumb. I give him a small smile, but we both know it's forced. "I know what you're thinking here, Sunshine, and you're wrong," he says, "you didn't cause this. You didn't put yourself or Rory in danger. Put the blame where it belongs, on that crazy fucker."

"I just wanna go home. I'm just so tired," I tell him.

"Ok, let's go," he climbs onto his bike and reaches out a hand to help me slide onto the seat behind him. I wrap my arms tightly around his waist and lay my head down on his back. I don't let go until we're safely back home.

twenty-two

Elijah

OVER THE NEXT FEW DAYS, the police touch base a few times with nothing new to say other than they're looking into every lead. I'm tired of hearing their bullshit excuses when I know how much is at risk here. I've been asking my buddy Breaker, the comms guys from our unit, to look into things for me and he should get back to me tonight. To the outside world, he seems like a respectable technical analyst and consultant. But in reality, he's an expert hacker. I'm sure there's a watch list somewhere around the world with several of his aliases on it, but they'll never track him down. He's an expert at covering his tracks.

Rory has taken the initiative on keeping Ember distracted and cheerful whenever she can, but I don't know how long she plans on staying. I'm not sure Ember or I could take losing her support right now. Tonight, the girls are sitting out on the deck enjoying the humidity, I'm sure. Every few minutes I hear one of them laugh loudly so I know they're a few bottles of wine into their night with no intention of slowing down. I'm perfectly ok with that. I've been busy for a few days working to complete a difficult design for a client who decided he wanted his first tattoo for his 70th birthday. In my opinion, it's never too late, so I'm happy to do it for him. My phone buzzes on the table next to me and I see Breaker's name flash across the screen.

"Hey man, what do you have for me?" I ask, not wasting any time with pleasantries.

"This guy is a fucking nightmare, man," he says, his voice sounding disgusted. I know whatever he found can't be good.

"Ok, spill," I say.

"His first year at Duke, he had five sexual assault reports filed against him that all magically disappeared because daddy made several large charitable donations to the alumni fund. That's just the tip of the iceberg, Elijah. I dug deeper and found his high school girlfriend. Apparently, she's the daughter of his father's business partner. She's currently in rehab for the second time after OD'ing on fucking downers. Seems like that started after she filed a police report when she was fifteen, accusing sweet Justin of breaking her arm in two places. The charges were quickly dropped, and she became a fucking ghost. It's like he leaves a trail of damage everywhere he goes," he says, taking a deep breath to calm himself down. We've always agreed that there's nothing worse on this planet than a man who takes advantage of those who are weaker than him. It seems my girl was just the next one in a long line of destruction for Justin.

"Did you find any accusations of stalking or any restraining orders? Anything that would imply he's done this to somebody else before?" I ask, clinging to the edge of my desk to keep from losing my shit.

"Nothing like that so far. It seems your girl is the first where that behavior is concerned. But there's a problem there, too. The report you guys filed about her Jeep getting fucked up is gone. It's like somebody erased everything. Why, I don't know. I tapped into his phone's text history and he's fucking at least three different sorority chicks right now, one of which is *barely* legal," he says in disgust.

"Any idea where he's hiding out?" I ask, barely keeping my composure.

"That's the thing, man. As far as I can tell, he's in Durham. He's still making steady payments on his apartment there. His spending history has all been local around that area. I haven't found much to suggest that he's anywhere near Grovewood," he says.

"What do you mean you haven't found much? Not much sounds like more than nothing," I reply.

"I pulled the security footage from the day Ember's Jeep got hit and it's just not clear enough to make out any details. Yeah, you can clearly tell it's a guy fucking up her shit, but you can't see his face or where he went after. He walks down a side street and disappears from any video footage," he says.

"FUCK!" I yell loudly, slamming my fist on my drafting table and swiping everything into the floor. I take a few calming breaths and when I pick my head back up, I see Ember and Rory standing by the back door, both frozen in confusion over my outburst. "Just keep at it and keep me posted with anything new," I snap at him and hang up the phone.

I stand up from my desk without a word and stomp upstairs into my room, slamming the door behind me. I don't like anybody to see this side of me. Sometimes I just have trouble keeping my temper under control. It's an attribute I always thought I inherited from my father. I pace back and forth across my bedroom, fury flooding through my veins at this helpless feeling. If I could just get my fucking hands on this guy, this would all be over. That's a life I would never feel guilt for taking. The rage and bitterness build throughout my body until I can no longer contain it. I slam my fist into the wall next to the bathroom, my hand disappearing into the drywall. I stare at the hole surrounding my wrist for several seconds before I feel a light touch on my arm. I turn and see Ember with tears in her eyes next to me. I didn't even hear the door open over the sound of the blood rushing in my ears.

"Eli, what have you done here?" She says, her face full of concern but her voice calm and soothing.

"I'm... I'm sorry. I didn't mean to scare you guys down there or do this. I just feel so fucking useless right now and all I want to do is protect you," I tell her, pulling my bloodied knuckles out of the wall.

"Come on, let's get this cleaned up." She takes my hand in hers and leads me into the bathroom. She directs me to sit next to the sink and turns the hot water on. I hold my hand over the drain to keep blood from dripping everywhere.

"Don't apologize to me, Eli. You did nothing wrong here," she says quietly.

"But I can't seem to track this fucker down, and I know you're terrified. It's my responsibility to make sure you're safe, Ember. To make sure you're happy. And I can't even do that," I say, knowing I sound a little like a pathetic child. I'm not trying to throw a pity party here, but I'm just so fucking angry. She pulls a rag out of the bathroom closet, runs it under the hot water, and begins to wipe away the blood and drywall dust from my fist.

"Elijah, I know you're doing everything you can to keep me safe. I love you so much for all you've already done to protect me. But I won't let you become another one of Justin's victims. I won't let the kind, loving man I fell for disappear because of this monster," she says, cradling my hand gently to her chest. She washes my hand clean and slowly kisses each of my knuckles. "He will not take what we have away from us. I won't let him." Her eyes are full of fire and determination. I smile up at her, loving the fierceness I see in her gaze.

"I love you, Sunshine," I say, feeling her thumb rub lazy circles over my already swelling knuckles. She bends down to place a soft kiss on my lips. I let her have a few moments of control before pulling her onto my lap and taking what's mine.

twenty-three

Ember

EVERYWHERE I LOOK IS BLACK. *I can tell my back is flat against something soft, but I see nothing, feel nothing around me. I beg my senses to find something to cling to, some hint of recognition in my surroundings. But it's no use. I'm alone. Suddenly, I feel a hand latch tightly around my ankle and I scream. A sinister laugh comes from the darkness. Slowly, the hand roams up my body, touching me roughly as I try to pull away. But my body is frozen in place. I thrash violently, but it's no use. I can't escape the touch of this ominous stranger.*

"Don't fight me, baby. You'll regret it," I hear a voice say, and I recognize it immediately. Justin's hands creep up my body, leaving a chilling trail in their wake. I try as hard as I can to pull myself from his grasp, but it's no use. My eyes, slowly adjusting to the darkness, catch a glimpse of the chains

surrounding my wrists and ankles. I pull against my bonds but make no headway in freeing myself from this prison.

"Oh, Ember, you knew better than to run. I'll always find you," he says, suddenly so close to my ear I can feel his breath against my skin. I jerk my head to the side, but his hand encircles my neck, halting my motion instantly. "You're mine, always mine," he says, squeezing his hand tightly around my throat. I pull franticly against my restraints, trying and failing to escape his grip. "Always mine," I hear him say as black spots dance across my vision. This is it, the moment my fight ends...

I sit up suddenly in bed, clutching my throat and coughing harshly. A small but desperate scream escapes my lips as the tears fall heavily from my eyes. Elijah's eyes snap open and he's up and out of bed, a pistol in his hand, before I can begin to process what's happening. He surveys the room, his eyes falling on my trembling form. He sets the gun on the desk by the door and comes back to bed, wrapping his arms tightly around me as I sob into his shoulder. His hands stroke my back softly as I cling tighter to him. These nightmares started slowly, only coming once a week when all of this started. Now they've become a nightly occurrence, and this is how we wake up each night.

"I'm sorry. I didn't mean to wake you. It's just becoming so much more... real, so vivid. It's like I can feel his hands on me," I tell him, taking several deep breaths to calm my racing heart.

"Don't be sorry, Sunshine. I know a thing or two about nightmares. It's okay, I'm right here. I'm not going anywhere. He will never touch you again, Ember," Eli says. He kisses my temple and I latch on to his torso, burying my head against his chest. I soak in a few more moments of comfort from him before climbing out of bed and walking to the bathroom.

I shut the door behind me and brace myself on the counter in front of the sink. I don't dare look at my reflection in the mirror. I hate the frightened little girl I see lately. She's defenseless and broken and I don't want to be her. I quickly strip out of my clothes and step into the shower, not bothering to wait for the water to warm up. The ice cold spray feels like thousands of needles against my skin and I let it sting. I don't care how much my skin aches from the frigid temperature surrounding me. I need to wash this feeling away. I'm tired of hiding, tired of looking over my shoulder every time I leave this house. I don't want to be the reason Elijah's first instinct is to grab a gun. Weak and feeble have never been words anyone would use to describe me. I won't let this asshole keep ruining my life.

All of a sudden, I'm engulfed in warmth. I was so wrapped up in my head I didn't hear Elijah come into the bathroom or slip into the shower behind me. He holds me silently for several long seconds before kissing my shoulder. I lean my head back against his chest, soaking in his love and strength.

"We're gonna be okay, Sunshine," he says softly.

"I know, honey." I turn and wrap my arms around his neck.

I push up on my tiptoes and kiss him softly. I step closer to him, pushing my body flush against him as his cock grows thick and heavy between us. I wrap my hand around his shaft, toying with his piercing and slowly sliding my hand up and down his silky skin until he groans. Moving my hand faster, I slide my palm over the sensitive tip. As we fight for control, I can feel the muscles throughout his body contracting. I make a move to drop to my knees, but he stops me.

"Not this time, baby. I need to be inside you," he says, his voice thick with lust. In one swift motion, he picks me up, wrapping my legs tightly around his waist and opening me up to him completely. He pushes my back against the cold tile wall and the contrast in temperatures makes me gasp. He teases me slowly, pushing inside my core with just the tip and pulling back out over and over until I'm clawing at his shoulders.

"Elijah, now," I say, sounding desperate and impatient.

He holds my body against the wall with his as he thrusts deeply, filling me completely in one stroke. I moan loudly, quickly adjusting to his size as if our bodies were made to fit together seamlessly. He stretches my walls so deliciously. I know I'll never get enough of this man. He moves, slow, shallow thrusts at first, then pounding into me as deeply as he can. I curl my fingers into his hair as his strokes become more intense. He bottoms out with each thrust, burying himself completely within me.

"Fuck, Sunshine. I could slide inside this sweet pussy every day and never leave," he says between strokes and heat flushes through my body at his words. I'm trying so hard to hold off my orgasm, wishing this feeling could last forever.

"I know you're holding back, Ember. I don't know why you even try. You're gonna fucking come for me, baby," he says, sliding his hand between our bodies and creating the perfect amount of pressure and friction on my clit to set me off. I detonate, my walls constricting around his cock in waves. I fist my hands in his hair, pulling so hard I'm sure he's gonna have a headache later. But I can't bring myself to care. He continues his punishing momentum, never letting up. I can feel another orgasm already building before I've even come down from the last one.

"Oh god, Elijah. Don't stop, please," I beg shamelessly.

"Never. I'll never stop, Em. God, I love you," he says, his icy blue eyes locking onto mine, pushing me over the edge again. I try to muffle my screams by burying my face into his neck as I explode, coming so hard I swear my vision blurs. He slams into me one final time, holding himself deep inside of me. I feel the heat of his release coating my walls, branding me as his. And I am his. I don't think I could even belong to anyone else again.

twenty-four

Elijah

I LEAVE Ember sleeping peacefully in my bed, her hair fanned out around her like a golden halo. The only time she sleeps soundly lately is after I've made her come so many times she can't keep her eyes open any longer. I definitely won't complain about that, though. I'll wear her out every day of the week, if that's what it takes.

There's no way I could go back to sleep after our 3am wake up call, though. She is having nightmares every time she closes her eyes, and I hate it. I head downstairs to grab some coffee and check in with Breaker. I know he'll be up this early. That asshole never sleeps. As I walk into the kitchen, I see two sets of eyes lock on mine and I jump.

"Jesus! You guys fucking scared me. What the hell are you doing up?" I ask. Everett and Rory are both sitting at the bar, looking like I just interrupted an intense conversation.

"Dude, I thought I gave you very explicit instructions when you told me you were gonna be fucking my sister. I distinctly remember saying 'as long as I don't hear you handling her', then I was cool with this situation. I really never needed to know that my sister is a screamer," he says, faking a gagging noise.

I genuinely laugh for the first time in what seems like forever. "I'd say I'm sorry, man. But I'm really, really not," I say with a smirk.

"Ewwww. No thanks," Rory says next to him, covering her ears like a child. "I can go the rest of my life without ever knowing a single detail of your sex life, bubba. Gross," she says with a shudder.

"Unfortunately, I was only responsible for one of those screams," I say, blowing out a frustrated breath. Rory's face falls, and Everett clenches his fists at his side. I pour a cup of coffee and scrub my hand down my face. "The nightmares are coming every night now."

"I'm so fucking done with this shit," Everett says, slamming his fist down on the bar.

"Is she okay?" Rory says quietly.

"She is now. She's sleeping, but I'm not sure how long that will last," I reply.

"What about Breaker? Has he found anything solid on this son of a bitch?" Everett asks, pushing away from the bar and pacing through the living room.

"Nothing good. This asshole is worse than she realizes. He's from old money, so mommy and daddy have bailed him out of so much shit. Honestly, he should be in prison by now," I tell him. He snatches his cigarettes off the edge of the table and storms out onto the deck, slamming the door behind him.

"What can we do here, Eli?" Rory asks, desperation in her voice. It warms my heart to know she cares so deeply for Ember already.

"I'm gonna reach out to Breaker again and see if he's been able to get a lock on Justin. I want to know exactly where he is. I think it's about time to give him a taste of his own fucking medicine," I say.

"I think you guys need to go do something fun today. She's been stuck in this house like a prisoner for days. It's not healthy, Elijah. Take her somewhere, just the two of you, and get her out of her head for a while," Rory suggests. It's really not a bad idea. We've both been so hung up trying to solve this clusterfuck of a situation, we've barely taken any time to just enjoy being together.

"Yeah, you're right, Bug. I think we'll get out of town for a little while this weekend. Hopefully, it'll be a nice mental break for both of us," I say, already knowing exactly where I'm gonna take her. I give my sister a kiss on the forehead and walk into the living room to call Breaker. He answers on the second ring, not sounding tired at all.

"What's the status, bro?" I ask.

"I think I found him," he says, sounding like he just got the high score on his favorite video game.

"What? Where?!" I ask, adrenaline already flooding my system.

"He's been in Charleston this whole fucking time. He's got some bitch back in Durham using his card, paying his bills, and driving his car just to make it seem like he's still there. But she signed her own name on a restaurant bill last night, the dumbass. Once I figured out she was the one using his shit, I tracked her cards and phone. Everything is in Charleston. I even found her car in the security footage from the clothing store where Ember's Jeep was parked. He used her card at the coffee shop next door an hour before Ember and Rory got there," he says. Finally, I feel like we have a solid lead on this guy.

"You're sure about this?" I ask, already knowing the answer.

"I'm insulted you would even ask me that, Elijah," he says, scoffing sarcastically. "Of course I'm fucking sure, asshole. I'm always sure."

"Thank you, Jason," I say, his real name sounding foreign coming out of my mouth. I've only said that once before when I needed him to know I was serious. "You have no idea how much it means to me."

"Of course. If she's important to you, then she's family, Elijah. Even if she wasn't Everett's sister," he says, his tone serious and genuine. "I'll send you everything I've found. Let me know if you need anything else." He hangs up before I can get another word in.

For the first time in weeks, I feel like we actually have something substantial to look into. I fill Everett in on everything I've learned and we agree to go soon to check out the address Breaker sent. It makes me uneasy to know it's only about fifteen miles from our front door. But today I'm not gonna dwell on that. I ask Everett and Rory to help me put my plan into motion, and they're both more than happy to help me make it happen. Today, I'm gonna wake up my woman and get her out of her head and out of this town for a few days.

twenty-five

Ember

I SIT in the passenger seat of my Jeep, picking at the hem on my cutoff shorts. When Eli woke me up, he told me to wear something comfortable and cool and be in the car in an hour. I love that he can still be spontaneous and adventurous amid all this drama. However, I've never been a fan of surprises. I'm a planner, I always have been. I like to make sure I'm prepared for anything by knowing all the details of a plan beforehand. Sensing my anxiety over being kept in the dark, Eli reaches over and takes my hand in his. He brings it up to his lips, kissing my knuckles softly.

"It's gonna be fun, Sunshine. I promise," he says with that perfect smile. When he smiles that way, I can't help but believe everything he says. I decide to let it go and enjoy whatever he has planned for the day.

"Can I ask you something?" I say.

"Anything," he replies, turning the music down.

"Why do you call me sunshine?" I ask, curious if he's gonna say something about my honey blonde hair reminding him of the sun. That's been my assumption, but now I want to know if I'm right.

"You wanna know the truth, or the most obvious answer?" He says, and I roll my eyes.

"The truth, obviously," I say. He takes a deep breath, like he's bracing himself to reveal a big secret.

"Because the first time I saw your face, it was like the sun began shining on me for the first time in years. You radiate this warmth and joy, even with everything you're up against. You pulled me into your orbit and I'll be happy to spend the rest of my life just soaking you in, Ember," he says, so matter-of-factly. I stare over at him with a watery smile, committing everything he just said to memory. He sees me in a way that I can't believe. I don't think I've ever felt so cherished or adored by anyone in my life. I feel the burn of happy tears building in my eyes and I will them away.

"I love you, Elijah," I say, my voice thick with emotion. Saying I love him doesn't even come close to expressing the way I truly feel about this man. He's the piece of me I never knew I was missing and I've never been so certain of anything in my life as I am about loving him.

"I love you too, Em. I never thought I would find someone that made me feel so... complete," he says the last part quietly, as if he's just now realizing it. He reaches over, laying his hand on my thigh and rubbing lazy circles over my skin. "Why don't you rest for a little bit, babe? We've got about an hour and a half of driving ahead of us and you're gonna want your energy when we get there," he says with a wink.

"You're not gonna give me a little hint? Not even a tiny one?" I ask, giving him the most innocent puppy dog look I can conjure up.

"Not gonna work, babe. My lips are completely sealed, at least for now," he says.

"Fine," I say, faking an annoyed huff. "I guess a nap doesn't sound terrible."

I turn on my favorite Indie music playlist and lean my seat back, settling in for the long drive.

I wake up when the Jeep comes to a stop, jostling me in my seat. I stretch my arms and legs out as far as I can in the tight space and crack my eyes open to take in my surroundings. The smell of the salt air drifting through the windows and the sounds of seagulls chirping overhead tell me we're close to the ocean.

"Where are we, honey?" I ask, looking at the beautiful beach condo we're parked next to.

"Holden Beach. We figured it was a good halfway point for both of us," he says.

"We? Who's we?" I ask, confused.

Elijah points out the front window towards the dunes in front of us. Standing on the walkway between the beach and the condo, I see a familiar raven-haired silhouette waving my way. I'm out of the Jeep and sprinting towards her without even taking the time to shut the door.

"Kelsea!!" I squeal as we launch ourselves into each other's arms, collapsing onto the deck in a heap of tears and laughter.

"Oh my god, Ember! You have no fucking idea how much I've missed you!" Kelsea says, squeezing me so tightly I can barely breathe, but I don't care. It's been months since I've seen my best friend and I don't want to let her go for even a second.

"How did you even get here?! How did you know we'd be here??" I ask, my mind running a hundred miles an hour.

"I got a phone call from a certain Blake twin this morning explaining the plan Elijah had in mind. I loaded my shit up in the car and hauled ass all the way here." She shrugs her shoulders like it's no big deal. "By the way, I've decided that I'm in love with your man. I mean, who plans something like this at the last minute and makes sure it all comes together so perfectly? That gorgeous man over there, that's who," she says, pointing back at Elijah as he leans against the front of the Jeep.

"Yeah, he's pretty incredible. But that one is mine, so

get your own," I say, laughing at Kelsea being Kelsea. We pick ourselves up off the ground and walk arm and arm back towards the driveway. I'm smiling so hard my face hurts, but I don't care. Having two of my favorite people together in one place feels amazing.

"Kelsea, it's nice to meet you in person," Eli says, reaching out his hand towards her. She laughs and wraps him in a hug in true Kelsea fashion.

"It's great to finally meet you, Elijah. I've heard *a lot* about you," she says with a wink, and I roll my eyes at her.

"I can only imagine," he says, laughing at us. He walks to the back of the Jeep, pulling two duffle bags from the trunk.

"You really covered all your bases here, huh?" I ask, touched that he put so much thought into what would make me happy.

"Well, I tried. Aurora packed your bag while you were in the shower, and she and Ev will be here in about an hour or so," he says, surprising me yet again.

"They're coming too?!" I ask excitedly.

"Yeah babe, they just stopped in town to grab some food for the weekend," he says.

"We're spending the entire weekend? Damn, if I had known, I would have grabbed my laptop. I have an edit due by tomorrow night," I say.

"It's in the bag, Em. I've got you covered," he says

with a smirk. God, I love this man more than words can express.

"You really are incredible, ya know?" I say, wrapping my arms around his neck and kissing his cheek.

"Oh, I know. You're really very lucky," he says, throwing me a sexy wink. I try to pull away, but he holds me tighter, kissing me deeper. He drops the bags and slides his hands up the columns of my neck. He tilts my head back, sliding his tongue into my mouth, and I moan softly. The entire world disappears when he kisses me this way.

"God damn, I'm glad I packed my vibrator," Kelsea says, pulling me out of the lustful daze I live in every time Elijah is near. He laughs against my lips and I feel my body heat with embarrassment.

"I think I'm really gonna like you, Kelsea," Eli says, wrapping his arm around my shoulder and leading the way to the door.

twenty-six

Elijah

"YOU'RE SUCH A FUCKING ASSHOLE, Everett Wayne!" Kelsea yells from across the house. Even though she, Everett, and Rory are out on the deck, we can still hear them perfectly with the sliding glass doors wide open. Everett's full-bodied laugh comes through loud and clear as Kelsea throws a peeled shrimp at his head. Ember and I carry the rest of the food out onto the patio table and settle in for dinner.

"How am I the asshole here, Kels? You're the one who walked out of the bathroom totally fucking naked! I just happened to be lying on my sister's couch at the time, enjoying her wonderful hospitality. I wasn't expecting to get dinner and a show when I went to visit my sister that night," Ev says, a devilish smirk on his face.

"A gentleman would have closed his eyes or something! You just fucking sat there staring at my tits like they were gonna do a damn magic trick or something," Kelsea says, laughing and rolling her eyes at Everett's recounting of his favorite Kelsea memory. I look over at Ember for some clarification and she just holds up her hands in surrender.

"I've never claimed to be a gentleman, baby. And I'd be a real fucking idiot not to appreciate the fine art you had on display there, Kels," Everett says, dodging another shrimp.

"Okay, okay, moving on, please!" Ember says, rolling her eyes at them both.

"I guess I'm glad I had a more subdued introduction to you then, Kelsea," I say, laughing.

"Has everyone here seen each other naked?" Aurora asks, her eyes wide and mischievous.

"Well, I try to stay away from Eli whenever he's naked, but he just can't get enough of this," Everett says, running his hand down his abs.

"Oh, you know it, pretty boy," I reply, blowing him a kiss that he pretends to catch and put in his pocket. This is exactly what I wanted when I decided we were gonna get out of town this weekend. Ember is completely relaxed, lying against my side with her head on my shoulder. We're all laughing and joking, just enjoying our time here without worrying about anything else. If we could stay here forever, I wouldn't complain. I look out towards the beach, the sun setting low over the waves, and I close my eyes. Pulling Ember in closer to me, I kiss her hair softly and breathe her in.

"I wish we could stay here and never leave," I whisper in her ear so only she can hear me. She looks up at me with those gorgeous green eyes and her beautiful smile.

"Me too, honey," she says quietly, wrapping her arms around my waist and squeezing me tighter.

"You wanna walk?" I ask, pointing down towards the water. She smiles wide and stands, holding out her hand to me.

"We're gonna walk for a while, guys," I say. "Don't let them kill each other, please Rory," I point between Kelsea and Everett.

"No promises," she says with a shrug.

We walk down the stairs and the long pathway leading to the sand. We both slip off our shoes and leave them behind, making our way down to the waterline.

"I've always loved the water," Ember says, swinging our hands back and forth slowly.

"Yeah? I had you pegged as more of a forest kind of girl," I say.

"I think I'd be happy with a little bit of both. Somewhere that I could get lost walking through the trees but also cool off in a creek or something when the Carolina humidity becomes killer," she says, bending down to pick up a broken sand dollar sticking out of the sand.

"Somewhere like the plantation?" I ask, trying to

keep my tone neutral. The last thing I want is to suggest something she's not ready for and scare her away.

"What do you mean, Eli?" she asks, stopping in front of me.

"Well, I've been meaning to tell you, but we've been so caught up. The renovations on the first floor are done. It's move-in ready whenever I am," I say and I see her face fall a little. She quickly masks her emotions and turns to keep walking ahead. I stay rooted in place with my hands in my pockets. How long will it take her to realize that I'm not following? I smile to myself, knowing there's no way I would ever leave without her by my side. But I'll let her continue with her phony attempt at pretending it doesn't bother her to think of me not living in the townhouse.

"Oh, well, that's awesome. I know you've been working really hard for that, so I'm so happy for you. At least we won't be four people crammed into that three-bedroom townhouse anymore," she laughs, but it's obviously fake. She turns to look at me when I don't reply, and I laugh at her softly.

"You're right, Sunshine. I think that townhouse is really more suited for two people," I say, hoping she'll take the hint.

"Oh," she says, sounding even more disappointed than before, "Rory's leaving too?"

I laugh loudly at that suggestion and she stares back at me, confused. "No, babe," I come closer to her and put my hands on her hips to pull her in to me. "Rory is taking over my half of the rent at the townhouse for now. She said she needs some distance from home and she likes it in Grovewood. Besides, if you remember correctly, there's only one bedroom on the main floor, and I'm definitely not sharing it with my sister." I slide my hands up her neck and tilt her head back so she's staring straight into my eyes. "There isn't anyone I would ever want to share my home with but you, Ember." She closes her eyes and smiles widely.

"Really?" she says, her voice quiet but excited.

"Absolutely. I mean, as long as you want to. You don't have to. You're more than welcome to stay living with your brother and a broken shower," I say, shrugging my shoulders.

She launches herself into my arms, kissing me hard. "No thanks, I prefer showering with you, anyway," she says with a seductive grin. I pull her lips down to mine, nipping at her bottom lip until she lets out a tiny moan. I pour every ounce of my love and devotion for my woman into this kiss.

"So, does that mean you'll move in with me?" I ask, breaking our kiss. She puts one finger to her lips, resting her elbow on the other fist, posing like she's thinking about something very seriously.

"On one condition," she says, holding up her finger.

"Name it," I say, knowing I'll do anything to make her happy.

"I get to decorate," she says with a playful grin that makes me laugh.

"Done," I say, wrapping my arms around her tightly, picking her up and kissing her as I walk us into the icy waves.

"ELIJAH, DON'T YOU DARE!" she screeches, which only drives me to move forward faster. She struggles against my grip, trying to get away. But it's no use, we're already waist deep and soaked.

twenty-seven

Ember

I DON'T KNOW how Elijah reads me so well. Even though our time together has only been a few months, I feel like he's always been a part of me. How he knew I needed Kelsea by my side right now, I don't know. I'm just so incredibly grateful he put this trip together, no matter how short it's going to be.

To anyone else, it may seem like a crazy idea to move in together so quickly. But for me, it's inevitable. We spend every night together already. Most of my wardrobe has made its way into his room, and we've already been technically 'living together' for months now. Now we'll just have the luxury of living together totally alone. As we make our way back towards to beach house, I find myself feeling completely at peace with my life and my decisions. Even though I still have plenty of doubts and fears about the situation with

Justin, I know Elijah would never let anything happen to me. I won't let Justin take away any more of my happiness.

We walk up the stairs leading to the back door, hand in hand. Now that the sun has set completely, the breeze coming off the water is chilling against my wet skin. Being kissed by the sexiest man alive in the waves? Definitely an incredible experience. However, the aftermath of jumping into the ocean fully clothed is not so fun. I shiver as Eli pulls me closer to his side, rubbing his hands down my arms to warm me up.

"Sorry, babe. I just got a little carried away," he says, and I know he's not really sorry at all.

"It's okay. I just didn't expect it to get so chilly. After the 90 degree heat all day, 75 feels ice-cold," I say, wrapping my arms around my body and rushing across the deck to the back door.

Everett, Rory, and Kelsea are all spread out on the large sectional in the living room watching some reality dating show. I know from experience, those shows are Kelsea's guilty pleasure, and Everett teases her mercilessly about them.

"Really guys?" I ask, not wanting to listen to the two of them bicker again. "You thought this was a good option for everybody?"

"Hey, Everett loves this show," Kelsea says, a playful smile spreading across her face.

Everett looks back at us, giving Eli a questioning

look, and Eli nods in return. Suddenly, Everett jumps off the couch, clapping his hands.

"This seems like a cause for celebration," Ev says, walking into the kitchen and pulling 5 shot glasses down from the cabinet. I can only assume he already knew what Elijah was going to ask me tonight.

"She said yes?" Rory says, leaning over the back of the couch excitedly.

"Woah, woah, woah, what am I missing here?!" Kelsea says from across the room. I see her gaze quickly flick to my left hand and back up to my face.

"Elijah asked me to move in with him," I blurt out, not wanting her to say out loud what I already know she's thinking.

"Oh," she says, turning back around to watch her show, "I thought you guys were already kinda doing that."

"I asked her to move in to *our place* with me, instead of sharing an apartment with these two," Elijah says, motioning to our siblings. The way he calls the plantation 'our place' brings me a sense of happiness I didn't know I was missing.

Everett starts singing the shots song from the kitchen and we all roll our eyes at him. The idea of taking a shot right now makes me feel a little queasy. Something about the rich seafood we had for dinner and the salt air around us has my stomach turning. Maybe I swallowed a little too much ocean water on our walk.

Whatever it is has me running to the bathroom. I barely make it before emptying the contents of my stomach into the toilet. After cleaning myself up, I sit down on the edge of the tub to relax for a second. Kelsea knocks on the door before coming in. She hands me my cozy pajamas and I change quickly as she grabs a washrag out of the closet and soaks it with cool water. Her face is full of concern as she hands it to me and I wipe my face, enjoying the refreshing feeling.

"What the hell was that?" She asks, plopping down onto the floor beside me.

"I don't know. My body and mind are just overwhelmed, I think. I've been trying to put on a good front for everybody else, so they don't worry. But I'm still freaked. I'm constantly looking over my shoulder every time I leave the house. The stress and anxiety of all of this is giving me nightmares, Kels. I've never felt so helpless in my life." I stand to wash my hands and face.

She steps beside me, pulling me in for a hug as we watch our reflections in the mirror. "You know what I see here?" she asks. I shrug, tears stinging my eyes.

"I see a woman who is strong, Ember. She's brave and capable. I know because she's taught me to be the same way over the course of our friendship." She gives me a small smile and I let the tears fall freely. "You may feel helpless now, but you're not. A helpless person would collapse under the weight of this pressure and you've never been one to quit. We're gonna get through this. That asshole is gonna get what he deserves, I promise you that," she says, squeezing my shoulder reassuringly.

"Thanks, Kels. I love you. I'm so glad you're here." I wrap my arms around her tightly. "I really have missed you so much. It's been a big change not seeing your face every day. But I'm sure Jake has been happier that he hasn't had to share you," I joke, wiping my eyes.

"Actually, we broke up," she says, her eyes dropping to the floor.

"What?! Why didn't you tell me?!" I ask.

"Because you have much more important shit going on here! I think creepy stalker trumps boyfriend problems any day of the week. Jake was a self-centered dick. I saw it in the beginning and I thought I could change him, which is incredibly stupid of me. Won't be making that mistake again," she says, shrugging like it's no big deal.

"Well, I still wish you would have told me. Your problems are just as important to me as mine are to you," I say, taking her hand in mine and squeezing it. She gives me a small smile, nodding her head. A knock on the door pulls us from our emotional moment.

"Hey, everything okay in there, Sunshine?" Elijah asks through the door. My smile widens at the sound of his voice.

"Yeah, we'll be out in just a second," I reply. Kelsea

looks me over with a grin that tells me she's got a lot to say about the man on the other side of the door.

"What?" I ask her, "just say it."

"I like him. He seems really good for you," she says. "When Everett called and suggested this weekend, I thought you guys were moving a little fast. But I can see why. He's amazing, Em, and you deserve the absolute best. Does he make you happy?"

I smile instinctively, thinking about all the ways Eli makes me feel happy and satisfied. "Yeah, he really does. When he asked me to move in with him tonight, I didn't feel a second of hesitation at all. I love him so much and I know he loves me. The world just seems right when we're together."

"Then that's all that matters, babe," she says with a smile. "Besides, there's no way a man can look that incredible and not have a big dick to back it up." I feel my body heat with embarrassment over her words, but I know she's not wrong. She takes my silence as confirmation, and we both dissolve into a fit of laughter.

twenty-eight

Ember

AS SOON AS I open my eyes the next morning, I feel my body dragging. It's as if it knows we have to return to reality today and it's starting a rebellion. In a perfect world, I would spend the rest of my days lounging on this beach, surrounded by all my favorite people. But this world is not perfect and reality always creeps its way in, whether we like it or not. I stumble my way through breakfast, only taking a few nibbles of toast. The air surrounding us is heavy with disappointment. Nobody wants to leave, and the feeling is tangible through us all.

The only good thing to come out of this morning is that my stomach seems to have settled over night. Unfortunately, I can already feel the anxiety building at the thought of returning home. Being able to leave the house and walk along the beach without being followed has been so relaxing. I make a point to remember to ask Elijah if he's heard anything new from the police or his hacker friend during the drive home. I want to start the next chapter of our journey together without this hanging over us. As we load the last of our things into the back of the Jeep, I can feel tears already welling up in my eyes and I try to wipe them away before anyone notices.

"Why are you crying, pretty girl?" I hear Elijah say as he walks up behind me and wraps his arms around my waist.

"Just sucks to have to say goodbye to Kelsea already. It feels like it's been forever since I've seen her. Even though I'm so grateful that you put all of this together, I wish we could have stayed longer," I tell him.

"I know, Sunshine," he says, kissing the side of my head. "I wish we didn't have to rush back, either. But we'll make sure the next visit lasts longer. Maybe she can come down soon and help you pick shit out for the house," he says and I nod my head, knowing there's few things Kelsea loves more than shopping.

"Alright, Thor. Hands off my woman," Kelsea says, pushing Eli away from me. She decided after our conversation last night that Thor was the most fitting nickname for him. I told him it was because of his build and longer hair, but I left out her comparison of his dick to

Thor's hammer. Sometimes that girl is just too much, but I wouldn't trade her for anything in the world.

We stand in silence, holding onto each other tightly for several long minutes. I hear her try to suppress a small sniffle, and I squeeze her tighter.

"Don't worry, Kels," I whisper, so only she can hear. "He takes care of me."

"I know. Otherwise, I wouldn't be letting you leave right now." She steps back and wipes her eyes. "Please be safe, sister. Don't make me have to kill this fine young man for letting something happen to you."

"It was great to finally meet you, Kelsea. I promise I'll keep her safe," Elijah says, wrapping her in a hug. She kisses him on the cheek and waves as she climbs into her car. As I watch the familiar taillights of her Subaru fade down the street, I feel like a piece of me is being pulled in her direction. I decide right then that I'm going to make it a priority to drive to Durham at least twice a month for some girl time. Orgasms are fantastic, but sometimes a girl just needs her bestie.

By the time we pull into the driveway back in Grovewood, I've had to make Elijah pull over three times for me to throw up. I don't know if it was the details Eli shared with me about Justin or something I ate, but I make an appointment with my doctor for tomorrow and decide to lie down for a nap.

The sound of the shower running pulls me from my dreams. I glance at the clock and see it's 7:30pm. I've been napping for almost five hours. I stretch my tired muscles and get out of bed, walking over to the bathroom to enjoy the show. Silently, I watch Elijah showering through a gap between the curtain and the wall. Does this seem a little voyeuristic? Maybe, but I don't care. My man is a sight to behold and I already feel moisture gathering between my thighs at the sight of him. I rub my legs together to try to relieve some of the ache, but that only makes me groan in discomfort. Elijah's eyes snap to mine and a wicked smile spreads across his face.

"You know you're always welcome to join me, Sunshine," he says with a cocky grin.

"Oh, I know," I reply. "I'm just enjoying the scenery for now."

"Is that right? You're sure you don't wanna come in?" He asks, gripping his shaft tightly in his hand and slowly stroking himself. I let out a small moan as I feel my nipples tighten at the sight of him bringing himself pleasure.

There are so many things that I never thought would turn me on until I met Elijah. I slide my hand up my torso, kneading my breasts and pinching my nipples lightly to relieve the ache. This only seems to turn him on more as he pumps his fist harder and faster, his eyes never leaving my body. I pull my shirt over my head and stand just out of his reach in nothing but my soaking wet panties and a sheer lace bra. He stretches out his arm to brace himself against the shower wall as I reach behind me and unclasp my bra, letting it fall to the floor.

"You're always sexy as fuck, Ember. But watching you touch yourself? Damn babe, I'm not gonna last long here," he says, his voice sounding gruff and strained.

"You mean like this?" I ask as innocently as possible as I slide my hand into my panties, slipping a finger between my folds. It glides effortlessly through my wetness and I rub small circles around my clit. I let out a breathy moan at the feeling of pleasure already building in my core. I watch Elijah stroke himself, rough and fast, and I wish it were my hands doing the work.

"Fuck, baby, if you keep looking at me like that, I'm gonna come," he says, his breaths coming in ragged pants as he tries to hold on to his control. I slide my panties down my legs and work a second finger through my wetness and into my core. The feelings are all too much. I feel the muscles in my body clench around my own fingers just as I see Elijah's knees buckle slightly and he explodes into his fist.

I'm still riding the high of my orgasm when I feel him pick me up, setting me down roughly on the edge of the counter. He drops to his knees without hesitation and lowers his head between my thighs, feasting on me like a starving man. My overly sensitive skin barely has time to adjust before I'm coming again. I wrap my hands around his head, shamelessly pulling him closer to me. My head falls back in sheer ecstasy as he pushes me over the edge. No one has ever owned my body the way he does. No one ever will.

twenty-nine

Elijah

THE NEXT MORNING, I have to be at the shop early. I slide out of bed, careful not to wake the angel sleeping next to me. Just when I think I can't possibly love her any more than I already do, I learn a new aspect of her personality and fall all over again. This woman will be my wife one day. I know that without a doubt. Whatever I have to do to make it happen, I'll do it. I give her a quick kiss, slipping out the door and downstairs silently.

The ride to the shop is always peaceful early in the morning. Most of the town hasn't woken up yet and I can just enjoy all the beauty South Carolina offers. Even though the loud pipes of my bike fill the air with noise, the town is still serene. I never regret choosing to build my life here.

I pull up in front of the shop and see our business manager, Helo, whose real name is Beckett, already inside, with several ledgers laid out across the front counter. Everett and I both hate doing the books and other administrative things necessary to run a business. When Helo was medically discharged from the Corps, he went through a dark time. For a lot of us, the Corps was all we had. It was our family, our purpose. Without that, he didn't know what to do with his life. After his mom called us one night to tell us he had tried and failed to end his own life, we knew we had to give him a new purpose. He was always a fucking genius with numbers and mechanics. I think that's part of the reason he became a pilot in the first place. Every time he climbed into the cockpit of his chopper, we knew our lives were in excellent hands. So Everett and I asked him to take over the financial and bookkeeping side of the business. He jumped at the chance, and for the first time in a long time, I saw a genuine smile on his face.

He's just one of many of our brothers in arms that have become an integral part of growing this business. With him controlling the financial side of things, Breaker taking care of all security or technical needs, and Iris, another of our brothers who earned his nickname from the saying 'I Require Intense Supervision', handling our legal dealings, we've kept our unit together outside the Corps.

I set a travel cup of coffee on the counter next to him and drop into a chair behind the desk. "How's it looking this month?" I ask.

"So far, so good. Business is up almost 80% more than this time last year. I think at this rate we're gonna have to look into buying the space next door to expand and maybe take on a few new artists just to keep up with appointments." Pride swells in my chest at what we've built here.

"Fuck yeah, dude. That sounds awesome. I'll call the real estate agent next week and start looking into it. Any big expenses coming down the pipeline this month?"

"Actually, yeah," he says, suddenly sounding nervous. "I didn't want to bother you guys during you trip, but we had a minor problem this weekend."

"What? What kind of fucking problem?" I ask.

"Breaker called me Friday night to tell me he lost connection with the security system. He asked if I could come in and reset the system. When I got here, all the cameras were down and the hardline that powers the system had been cut. Obviously, it was intentional and I'm sure we all have an idea of who could have done it. Replacing the cameras and rewiring the system won't be cheap, though. Breaker said now is a good time to upgrade the system if we're replacing shit, anyway. All in all, it's gonna run us around 10k to get things up and running," he huffs out a frustrated sigh. I feel my blood boiling under the surface of my skin. This motherfucker is messing with the wrong man. As if threatening my woman wasn't enough to want to end his life, now this asshole is fucking with my business. There are people who depend on me to keep their bills paid. I won't let him interfere with that.

"Did you call the cops and file a report?" I ask, rubbing my hands over my face, trying to clear my head.

"Yeah, of course. But you know how useful they've been so far," he says sarcastically.

"Do it. Whatever Breaker says we need to do to upgrade the system, just do it." I say, my tone clipped. He nods and closes the books in front of him. "Any other wonderful news you want to share?" I ask dryly.

"That's all I have for you today, boss. How is Ember holding up?" He asks, his voice full of genuine concern. Although I hate the circumstances, I'm glad she's managed to weave herself into my life so seamlessly.

"I think she's okay. She's a strong woman, but I know all of this is taking a toll on her. I was tempted to just stay at the beach on a permanent vacation," I scoff.

"From everything I've heard from you and Ev, she seems like a really good person. I hate to see this happening to her," he says.

"You and me both, brother," I say, clapping him on the shoulder and heading out the front door. "Let me know if you have any issues with the security system. I'll fill Ev in on everything." I climb on my bike, checking my watch. The jewelry store across the square is just opening its doors for the day. I've got a stop to make before heading back home. I think I take the long way back and clear my head.

thirty

Ember

WHEN I FINALLY WAKE UP, I'm alone with a splitting headache. I shuffle into the bathroom and splash some cold water on my face, hoping to liven myself up a bit. I feel my stomach turn and I barely have time to make it over to the toilet. What the hell did I catch? I'm rarely ever sick, but when I am, I feel like death. I want to crawl back under the covers and sleep until I feel human again. But I know I have a doctor's appointment in about an hour, so I take a quick shower, put on my comfy yoga pants and a t-shirt and head downstairs. Rory is sitting at the bar, scrolling through job postings on her laptop. She turns to wave, but her face drops when she sees me.

"Good god, you look terrible," she says.

"Thanks so much, love you too, Aurora," I say lightheartedly.

"I mean... that's not what I meant... you just look like you *feel* terrible is what I meant," she says, trying not to hurt my feelings.

"Oh, I know. I feel worse than I look, trust me. I made a doctor's appointment so I'm hoping Eli will be back in time to take me because I'm so exhausted and I'm not trying to crash my Jeep," I say, lying my head down against the cool granite countertop.

She pulls her t-shirt up over her mouth and nose like a make-shift mask. "Keep your germs to yourself, girl! I have a job interview later and I cannot be sick," she says, backing away from me.

I laugh and fake a cough in her direction. "Oh no, better stay away," I say, inching closer to her. She grabs her coffee cup and takes off upstairs, running into her room and slamming the door. I laugh, sliding into her chair and eating the toast she left on her plate. I hear the garage door open, signaling Elijah's return, but I don't budge. The two small bites of toast have already threatened to revolt, and I don't want to risk moving. He comes into the kitchen, tossing his bike keys onto the table by the door and coming straight to my side.

"Babe, you look awful," he says, kissing my head gently. He holds his hand up to my forehead to check for a fever and the cool temperature of his skin is so soothing.

"Yeah, I feel worse. I'm pretty sure I've got the flu.

Hopefully, the doctor will be able to give me something to help me at least keep some food down," I say, leaning into his shoulder. "This is probably a bad time to reveal that I have doctor phobia, huh? I almost want to say fuck it and go back to bed."

"It's gonna be fine. I'm going to be there the whole time," he says, gently pulling me off the stool and guiding me out to my Jeep. He helps me into the passenger seat, buckling my seatbelt before walking around to the driver's side. Sometimes the little things he does to take care of me are just too adorable. I can't imagine any other guy taking the time to make sure my seatbelt was buckled before pulling out of the driveway.

By the time we pull into the parking lot at the clinic, my anxiety is through the roof. I wish I could say I had some traumatic experience in a doctor's office as a kid and that's why I feel this way, but I didn't. I've just never liked them. Before I can plan my escape, Elijah is opening my door and helping me down. He grips my hand tightly all the way inside and while I check in. We take our seats in the waiting room and he continues to brush his fingers across my knuckles reassuringly.

"It's ok, Sunshine," he says, kissing my head. "It's just a little bug. They can give you something to help you feel better and we can go home and get back in bed." I smile up at him because that sounds like heaven.

"Ember Blake?" The nurse calls from the door. My

eyes dart to Elijah, but he exudes a calming energy that is almost infectious. Almost. We walk through the doorway and she takes my vitals quickly, then directs us to the exam room.

"Ok, I have to ask you some personal questions now, Ms. Blake. Are you okay with your husband staying in the room?" She asks.

"Oh, I'm not -" Elijah begins to say something, but I interrupt him. There's no way he's leaving me alone in this room.

"Yes, he can stay," I say, grabbing his hand and squeezing it tightly. He beams over at me with that beautiful smile of his and I realize she just called him my husband and I didn't let him correct her. Honestly, it felt completely natural and I actually kinda like the sound of it.

"Ok, no problem," she continues. "How long have your symptoms been going on?" She asks.

"I guess about a week now. I've been having headaches and feeling tired for about a week. The nausea and vomiting just started," I reply.

"Ok. Are you sexually active?" She asks.

Elijah barks out a laugh next to me, and I roll my eyes at his outburst.

"I'll take that as a yes," she says, smiling at me humorously. "When was your last menstrual cycle?" She asks, and suddenly the air is sucked out of the room. My periods have always been irregular, so I've never really thought to keep track of them. I know I'm horrible at remembering to take my damn pill, but I've tried to be more careful. I count back the weeks since my last cycle and realize I've missed one entirely and I should be in the middle of one again right now. But I'm not. That's almost 10 weeks since my last cycle. All the blood drains from my face and my body feels flush and heavy all at once. I know the nurse and Elijah are both staring at me, waiting for my reply.

"Babe, you okay? You look like you're gonna pass out," he says, but his words barely register. I look over at the nurse and she looks at me with knowing eyes.

"It's been about... 10 weeks." I whisper, as if I don't want to believe it myself. I look over at Eli and I see the exact moment he connects the dots. His eyes convey his shock and he squeezes my hand tightly before schooling his features completely. His emotions become unreadable, which brings me even more confusion and panic.

"Ok," the nurse says calmly, "we'll need a urine sample then, so we can run the test." She leaves to gather the supplies and shuts the door.

I nod my head absently, already knowing what the outcome will be. I can't believe I didn't realize it before now. My hand instinctively drops to my flat stomach and Elijah's eyes follow. We both sit in complete silence, neither of us daring to moving or speak.

"I love you," Elijah says, breaking the silence. I look over at him and see his focus is still on my stomach. That brings a small smile to my face. Maybe he won't freak out and run. This isn't at all what he signed up for, but it's too late to turn back now. All I know for sure is by the time we leave here, we won't be the same people we were this morning.

thirty-one

Elijah

FEAR AND UNCERTAINTY flood my brain. Ember comes back from the bathroom and the nurse tells us the doctor will be here in about ten minutes. Is it possible to be both terrified and elated at the same time? I know this wasn't the plan. This definitely wasn't something we were trying for or even discussed. Hell, I never even considered having kids in the first place. But I can't help but feel giddy and excited to know the results. Panic creeps in as I realize Ember doesn't know anything about what I did this morning. I have to tell her. If I wait, she's gonna assume the worst and I need her to know I mean it and that my intentions are sincere, no matter what the outcome of this appointment is.

"I have to tell you something," I say, a little louder and more aggressively than I intended to. She turns her body to face me full on, her anxiety written all over her face. "I did something this morning. I wasn't gonna tell you until we got settled in the new house and got our own routine going. But I feel like I have to tell you now because I want you to understand I'm not with you out of any obligation. No matter what the result of that test is, I love you, Ember. I know you're it for me. You're the one who makes me want to be better and do better just to make you smile. I'm going to love you in your weakest moments, when you feel like breaking. And I'm gonna love you when you're strong, because damn, you are so strong. I'll be here loving you, no matter what comes our way. Each and every piece of you, for the rest of my life." I see a tear slide down the side of her face, but she doesn't make a move to wipe it away. "I want you to know I'm ready for whatever comes next, no matter what it is. But I won't take this step if it isn't what you want right now. I just needed you to understand that I was ready before today's surprising turn of events," I say, placing the decision in her hands.

She closes her eyes, taking a deep, calming breath as a smile spreads across her beautiful face. "Just so I know we're on the same page here, are you asking me to marry you, Elijah?" She asks without opening her eyes, as if she believes opening her eyes will make this moment disappear. I slide the ring box I picked up this morning out of my pocket and hold it in front of her.

"Open your eyes, Sunshine" I say, suddenly nervous about her response. Her perfect forest green eyes lock onto mine, not daring to look down. "Yes, Ember. I'm asking you to marry me," I say with confidence. She finally looks down and takes in the delicate emerald and diamond ring I'm holding in my hand. Her hands cover her mouth as she gasps, and I know I did good. I see the tears falling freely from her eyes as she stares down at the ring for several long seconds before meeting my eyes.

"One question," she says, "I just need to be clear on something. You're not just doing this because you probably knocked me up, right?" She asks, a sarcastic grin on her face.

"No, baby, that would just be a bonus," I answer without hesitation. Instantly, she takes the ring from my hands and slides it onto her finger. Before I can think, she's kissing me. I pull her out of her chair and onto my lap to kiss her back the way she deserves to be kissed. Are we making out in a doctor's office? Absolutely, and I don't fucking care who sees us. This is my woman. Soon, she'll be my wife. And I'll never be ashamed to show anyone exactly how I feel about her. I thread my fingers through her hair, angling her head so I can slide my tongue into her mouth. The cinnamon taste I love so much explodes on my tongue, and I let out a gruff moan. I know we have to stop before my cock rips a hole in these jeans, but there's something about this woman that I can never get enough of. She pulls away slightly, leaning her forehead against mine and smiling widely.

"Did that really just happen?" she asks in a soft whisper.

"Yeah, Sunshine," I say, placing my hands on either side of her face and pulling her in for a gentle kiss. "You're mine forever now."

We're interrupted by the sound of the doctor clearing her throat from the doorway. Ember scrambles to stand up off my lap and I just laugh. She smooths her hands down the legs of her jeans, that sexy crimson blush spreading up her chest and across her cheeks.

"I'm so sorry," she says, sitting back down in the chair beside me.

"I'm not," I say, shrugging my shoulders. She punches me in the arm, making me laugh even harder.

"Oh, trust me, I've seen far worse in this office," the doctor replies. "Besides, when you're in love, you're in love. And it's so clear that you two love each other." Her compliment makes me smile. I'll do whatever I have to do to make sure the entire world knows how much I love this woman.

"We didn't mean to get so carried away," Ember says shyly beside me. She reaches over for my hand and I can tell she's nervous about what the doctor has to say. I'm a little on edge too, but I know either way, we're gonna be okay.

"Oh, don't worry, you'll be feeling that a lot more often over the next few months. Pregnancy hormones are no joke," the doctor says with a grin, laying the positive test results on the table in front of us.

thirty-two

Ember

IF SOMEONE TOLD me I would be leaving the doctor's office today with an engagement ring and an ultrasound picture, I would have called them insane. Yet here we are, silently sitting in the Jeep, just staring at the little bean we created. Watching the tears gather in Elijah's eyes as the doctor played the sound of our baby's heartbeat was a moment I'll never forget. I love this man, and I know he loves me. Together, we're going to love this baby better than our parents ever loved us.

"She kinda looks like a gummy bear," Elijah says. I snatch the ultrasound picture from his hand, glaring at him.

"She does not! And you don't even know that she is a she. She could be a he," I look down at the picture and feel myself wanting to cry all over again, which I've learned is something else I'll have to get used to in the coming months. "Whatever they are, he or she is perfect," I breathe.

I was never one of those girls that daydreamed about getting married and filling my house with babies. There's nothing wrong with wanting that at all, but it just wasn't my dream. I spent more time dreaming about the library from Beauty and the Beast and wanting to be surrounded by piles and piles of books. I wanted to know I introduced the world to an amazing author or story. But right now, all I can imagine is reading all my favorite classics to my own baby. We drive back home talking about all the things we have to get done before the baby gets here. Hopefully, we can be fully moved in to the plantation by then and not have to bother Rory and Everett with a screaming baby at 2am.

As we pull into the driveway, I see Everett's bike parked next to Eli's, and I know he's home. I feel myself becoming anxious at the thought of telling my brother the news. Will he think we've moved too fast? I would never want to cause a rift in his and Eli's friendship.

"If you would prefer to wait before we tell them, we can do that. Whatever you want to do, Ember, I'm with you," Elijah says. I don't know how this man always reads my mind, but he does. No matter what happens, he will always have my back, and that feels amazing. I look down at the stunning ring on my left hand. The center stone is a beautiful pear cut emerald with diamonds branching out on either side like vines. It's incredible and unique, something I would have picked for myself. I know I made the right choice in saying yes, and I don't want to hide my joy from the people I love the most.

"Let's go tell Uncle Ev the good news," I say, smiling and climbing out of the car.

We walk in to the sound of rock music blaring from the sound system in the living room. I know from years of experience that means Everett is in a bad mood.

"Uh oh," Elijah says, picking up the same vibe I did, "wonder what crawled up his ass today," He shouts over the music.

"You'd think he'd pick something else after 15 years, but I guess not." I roll my eyes as Elijah turns down the stereo to a reasonable level.

"Hey! What the fuck!" I hear Everett yell from his room. He comes storming out, stopping short when he sees us. "Oh, sorry, I didn't think you guys would be back for a while," he says, obviously irritated about something.

"The Foo Fighters, Ev? Still?" I ask, remembering the same songs blaring from his room when we were in high school.

"Don't worry, I won't tell Dave Grohl you were talking shit, Sparky," he says with a smirk.

"What's got you in your angry feels, brother?" Eli asks him.

"Nothing, just fucking women, man. They're insane.

And I'm also pretty pissed about shelling out 10k for something so fucking stupid," he says and I twist my face in confusion.

"What? What do you have to spend that much money on?" I ask.

"You didn't tell her?" He asks Eli.

"Not yet. I didn't really get the chance to before we had to go to the doctor," Eli says, sounding a little guilty.

"Tell me what? What's going on?" I ask, throwing my hands up in annoyance.

"Justin. He fucked up some shit at the shop. Cut the hardline for our security system and broke a bunch of cameras," Everett says, and my stomach falls. It's one thing to mess with me, but now he's going after the people I care about most. He's affecting their lives and their business. When will this nightmare end?

"I'm so sorry, you guys. Sometimes I think I never should have come here," I say, sitting down at the bar and dropping my head into my hands.

"Don't you fucking say that," Elijah snaps, but I don't raise my head to look at him. "You belong here, Ember. You belong with me. How do you not see that by now?" he asks.

"What I see is all the trouble I've brought into your life, Elijah. I see all the danger I've brought to your doors," I say, his attitude irritating me. My emotions are already on edge after today's events and the hormones don't help the situation.

"You think I give a fuck about some cameras and a security system, Ember? Ten grand is nothing compared to knowing you're safe," he says. Usually his alpha male protective vibe turns me on, but today I'm exhausted, pissed off, and I don't have the patience to be rational.

"You don't get it, Eli. If I hadn't come here, none of you would be in danger at all. None of this would even be happening. He could really hurt someone, and that would be my fault." I know I'm screaming at him by now, but I don't care. The fire inside of me has taken over and I can't control the fury I feel.

"Ember, that's not fair," Everett adds. "No matter where you went, I would have been there. I never would have let you go through this shit alone, even if you didn't move here."

"You know what? I didn't fucking ask either of you for help. I wanted to do everything I could to keep you all safe, but that doesn't matter to either of you. You both want to swing your dicks around and talk about how 'you're doing everything for my protection', but you're not. Because we all know the safest option would be if I wasn't here at all," I say, turning and going upstairs into my old room and slamming the door behind me. I know I'm being childish and unreasonable, but I'm scared. I'm scared for the people who matter the most to me. I don't know how I would survive if something happened to any of them. The guilt would tear me apart for sure.

I see Kelsea's name flash across my phone screen, lying next to me. It's like she has a sixth sense for when I'm in distress. Even though I'm angry at Elijah and my brother right now, I still want to share all the news from my day with her. I pick up the phone with a small smile.

"Hey Kels, how is it you always know exactly when I need to hear your voice?" I say with a laugh.

I hear a familiar but sinister voice come through the line and my blood runs ice cold. "Oh my love, I have always known what you needed," I hear Justin's low voice say. I'm frozen in fear. How is he calling me from Kelsea's phone? Where is she?

"Where is Kelsea, Justin?" I ask, trying my best to hold it together.

"Your little bitch of a best friend is fine. For now, at least. We're just getting to know each other a little better, aren't we, Kelsea?" I hear a muffled voice in the background, and tears spring to my eyes. Adrenaline and terror are flooding my system at the thought of what could be happening to her.

"What the hell are you doing? What do you want?" I ask.

"You know what I want, Ember. All I've ever wanted was you. I would be willing to look past your transgressions if you would just come to your senses and realize that," he says, his voice sounding manic. After learning everything Elijah told me about Justin's past, I know he has the potential to hurt Kelsea, if he hasn't already. I have to be careful with how I play this situation so I don't set him off.

"You're right, Justin. It's so generous and understanding of you to give me a second chance," I say, trying my best to sound genuine.

"I've always given you more liberties than I should when it comes to your behavior, Ember. That will have to change," he says, scolding me like a child.

"Of course," I reply, trying to keep the disgust from coming through in my voice. "I understand completely."

"Why don't you come back to me and we can discuss things? You shouldn't have any trouble finding me. I've made sure to take care of your place for you," He says.

"My old place?" I ask, confused as to why he would be there.

"Our place, my love. I was willing to look past all the damage and imperfections when the landlord showed it to me. It was easy to get it back for us," he says, as if he's done me a favor.

"How... thoughtful of you," I say as my stomach turns at the thought of how he's infiltrated my life. He's taken some of my favorite places, my favorite memories, and twisted them into nightmares.

"Come to me now, Ember, and Kelsea can leave. I only needed her as leverage to help you behave, anyway. She's useless to me otherwise," he says, a threatening tone in his voice. I shudder to think what he could do to her if he sees her as useless.

"I'll come. I just need some time. After all, it's a long drive," I say, trying to buy myself some time to think of a plan.

"You have two hours. If you say anything to your brother or that disgusting trash you've been slumming with, I'll kill her. She doesn't matter to me at all, Ember, and it wouldn't be the first crime I've gotten away with," he says with a laugh. I feel the tears pouring from my eyes as I try to keep my composure. Two hours will be nearly impossible, but I have no choice. I place my hand over my belly, knowing I have more than just my life to consider.

"I'll be there. I'm leaving now, Justin. Just don't hurt her," I beg. I hear a struggling sound on the other end, followed by Kelsea's voice yelling.

"Don't fucking come here, Ember! Stay away!" she screams and I hear a slap. Then all is silence. I'm sobbing in fear for her as I throw my keys into my bag and slide my shoes on.

"Justin, please! Please, just leave her alone! I'm coming now. Just don't hurt her," I beg him.

"She'll learn her place some day," he says. "I'll see you in two hours, my love." He hangs up abruptly, and I release the sobs I've been holding back.

Tears cloud my vision as I gather my stuff and try to pull myself together. I wipe my face and sling my bag over my shoulder. I force the steel into my spine and walk downstairs. Elijah and Everett are bent over a computer at the bar. They both turn when I walk by and look at me with concern.

Before either of them can say anything, I hold up my hand. I know if they speak, I'll break and I can't afford to do that right now. "I'm going to go out for a bit. I need some space to clear my head and calm down. It's not up for negotiation," I say, hoping my false confidence is enough to keep them from asking questions.

"I wish you wouldn't go out alone, Sunshine," Eli says, "I understand you need space. Will you at least meet up with Rory? She just finished her interview at the coffee shop, so she's still in town." I nod my head silently. I make my way over to him, wrapping my arms around him. My composure is barely there, but I can't leave without making sure he knows how I feel. The idea that I might not make it back to him breaks my heart, but I have no choice. I won't let Kelsea suffer for me.

I kiss him softly, pulling him flush against my body. "I love you, Elijah. So much. Don't forget that," I tell him, not daring to look him in the eyes.

"I love you too, Em. I'll be here when you get back," he says. Before I can change my mind, I give him a forced smile and walk out the door. I climb into the Jeep, take a deep breath, and pull out of the driveway. I don't have any more time to waste.

thirty-three

Elijah

I UNDERSTAND why Ember is pissed, but I can't bring myself to agree with her. I know she thinks she's responsible for all of this bullshit. But she's not, and I won't let her take the blame. If I didn't want to kill the fucker, I'd thank Justin for pushing her here. We may not be in the position we're in right now if he hadn't, and I'm thankful for that.

"You're gonna regret siding with me," Everett says, slapping me on the back.

"Probably, but I'm not sorry. I love her more than I've ever loved anyone in my life, Ev. I won't be sorry for anything that brought her to me." I know I should like a Lifetime movie, but I'm confident enough in myself that I don't care.

"I'm glad you two found each other," Everett says, grabbing a Red Bull from the fridge, then leaning against the counter and crossing his arms. "I was a little weirded out about it in the beginning because I never wanted to think about my best friend fucking my sister. I still don't. But I can tell you really love each other and you both deserve to have that in your lives."

"Thanks, bro. It makes me happy to hear you say that. Especially since I asked her to marry me," I say calmly, and he chokes on his drink. I can't help but smirk at his surprise.

"I'm sorry, you did what?!" He says between coughs.

"I asked her to marry me. And she said yes." I say, looking him straight in the eyes. His gaze is burning a hole through me, but I won't back down. Ember is mine and nothing he says will change that.

"Are you serious?" He asks, masking his emotions seamlessly.

"Yeah, I am. I'm in this with her forever, no matter what comes our way. She's made me a better person, a stronger person. I've never wanted to look too far into the future. I've been content floating through life with no real direction or purpose. But as soon as I saw her, it's like my world snapped into place," I say, smiling at the thought of this morning's events. "I didn't want to tell you like that. I wanted Ember to tell you how ever she decided was best. But we're both in the doghouse now." He stares back at me as if he's deciding how to feel about this situation. While I want his blessing and approval in this, I don't need it. It won't change how I feel.

He looks away, staring into space like he's reaching for a distant memory. "You'll take care of her," he whispers. It's a statement, not a question. There's no question. He knows I will.

"Always," I reply. He nods his head before a smile spreads across his face.

"I'm happy for her. She deserves somebody who treats her like the amazing person she is. You, not so much. I mean, I guess I'm happy if you're happy. But you're gonna willingly commit to be with her forever? You might need to have your head examined," he says, laughing loudly. I roll my eyes and laugh. The front door opens and closes and I'm hoping Ember changed her mind about staying out or maybe she caught up with Rory and talked it out.

Rory comes into the kitchen alone and sets her bag down on the bar. "Hello, ladies," she says, heading straight to the fridge.

"Hey Bug, how'd the interview go?" I ask.

"Good. I start next week so I'm gonna sleep in every day this week before I can't anymore," she says.

"Did you calm my sister down?" Everett says, and Rory looks at him with a confused expression.

"What do you mean? Why would I need to?" She asks looking between him and I.

"We all kinda got into it. She said she was going into town to meet you. You didn't see her?" I ask, feeling my anxiety creeping in.

"I didn't talk to her. She wasn't in town either. You sure she was coming to meet me?" Rory asks, and I feel my adrenalin already spiking.

"Yes, Aurora. She said she was meeting you at the coffee shop. You're sure you didn't see her?" Everett asks, panic coming though in his voice.

"I'm sure, guys. I didn't talk to her or see her," she says. I already have her number pulled up in my phone and I try calling her. It rings several times before going to voicemail. I hang up and try again. Voicemail.

"Everett, call her. Maybe she's just that pissed at me," I say, hoping that's the case. He raises the phone to his ear, his brows knit together in confusion. He shakes his head as I hear the faint sound of her voicemail message on his end. I know something is wrong. I can feel it in my bones. I look over at Rory and see she's already calling her too, but she gets no answer.

"What the fuck?" Everett says, "Why wouldn't she answer? Where would she go?"

I scroll through my contacts and find Breaker's number. What I'm about to do may piss her off, but I don't care. He answers on the first ring as usual, "What's up, brother?"

"I need you to track Ember's phone. Now," I ask, not wasting any time with formalities.

"You sure about that? I can do it but - " he starts but I interrupt him. I don't have time for his hesitation.

"I'm sure, do it now." I say aggressively. He pushes several keys on the other end of the line.

"What the fuck?" He mumbles.

"What? Where is she?" I ask.

"She's on the highway heading towards Durham," he says.

"I'll call Kelsea. Maybe she just needed to get away," Everett says, dialing Kelsea's number. I see anger in his features when her phone goes to voicemail as well.

"Track this number, Breaker," I tell him, rattling off Kelsea's cell number.

"That's fucking weird. She's in Ember's old apartment building. Hold on," I hear Breaker say, the sound of him typing furiously coming through the speaker.

"Why would she be there?" I ask, not expecting him to really know the answer.

"We have a fucking problem, Elijah. I put a tracer on the phone Justin's been using a while back just to keep tabs on the fucker. His location and Kelsea's are pinging right next to each other," he says. I feel my blood run cold. From the corner of my eye, I see Everett dialing Kelsea again and again, but she doesn't answer.

"Ember wouldn't do this, right? She wouldn't go there alone, would she?" Rory asks quietly, fear evident in her voice.

"She would for Kelsea," I say, the pit in my stomach twisting tighter and tighter at the thought of her being anywhere near Justin.

"FUCK!" Everett throws his phone across the room, letting his anger get the best of him and smashing it against the wall. "Where is my fucking sister, Breaker?" He yells.

"I'll send you her location now, but she's got about an hour and a half head start on you guys. She's only about 45 minutes away from them," he says as my phone lights up with his message.

"Keep your eyes on them. See if you can tap into the building's security cameras and keep us posted," I say, hanging up on him.

I climb the stairs two and a time, grab my pistol from the bedside table, slide it into the holster at my back and we're out the door in seconds. Everett and I can ride faster than we could drive in the highway traffic. My mind races with thoughts of everything that could happen before we can get to them. I think about the tiny heartbeat I watched flickering on the ultrasound screen this morning. Why would Ember take this risk?

Rory stays behind, just in case, with the promise that we'll keep her posted on what's going on. I just hope Ember can hold her own until we can make it there.

thirty-four

Ember

I PULL to a quick stop in front of my old building, not caring that I'm parked in a fire lane. Let them give me a ticket. At least then I would know the cops were around. I look up to the window that used to lead into my living room. That building has been the setting of some of my most treasured memories. Now, it's poisoned by my imagined images of Kelsea suffering somewhere inside.

I race into the building, not even bothering to lock the doors of my Jeep. On a normal day, I would wait for the antique elevator to carry me up to the third floor, but I don't have time to waste tonight. I take the stairs two at a time, trying to keep my racing heart under control. By the time I make it to the door of the apartment, I'm sucking in breaths rapidly. My lungs burn from the exasperation, but I pull myself together.

I pound my fist against the door and listen for any

movement coming from inside. "Justin!? I'm here! Open the door! Please! Kelsea?" I yell, beating my fist against the door so hard I can hear the chain rattle against it from the other side. Suddenly, the door swings open and someone grabs me by the elbow, pulling me inside quickly and pushing my back against the door as it slams shut.

"What the fuck are you doing, Ember? Trying to wake the entire building?" Justin says, his face only an inch or two away from mine. I feel his hot breath against my cheek and a knot forms in the pit of my stomach. I've never before been so disgusted by someone's touch as I am right now.

"No! I'm sorry, Justin. Really, I was just in such a hurry," I say, trying to pull my arm from his grasp, but that only makes him squeeze tighter. I know I'll have a few finger-shaped bruises there tomorrow, if I make it to tomorrow. The look in his eyes is unlike anything I've ever seen outside of horror movie villains. His usual brown irises are nearly black. His expression is so cold and empty, it sends a shiver up my spine. I've seen him mad. In fact, I've been both the cause and target of that anger, but I've never seen him this disconnected from reality. "You're hurting my arm, Justin," I say as calmly as possible.

He continues staring into my eyes, a sinister smile spreading across his lips. "Sometimes, my love, a little pain is necessary. You didn't appreciate that before. But you will now," he slowly releases his grip one finger at a time. He shoves me down onto the couch, and I pull my knees tightly up to my chin. I don't want to say or do anything to anger him further, but I'm terrified. I can't tell from across the room that his pupils are the size of saucers, telling me he's obviously on something. We sit in motionless, me staring at the floor, him staring at wall blankly. I want to ask about Kelsea, but I don't want to set him off. The cavern of silence between us grows wider by the minute. After nearly an hour and a half just sitting here, I can't take it anymore.

"Justin," his eyes snap to me instantly, and they're completely vacant. Like there's no one actually inside his body. "Where is Kelsea?" I ask, looking around the living room and kitchen. I don't see any sign of her, but I feel bile rise in my throat when I spot a small pool of blood on the kitchen floor. "Oh, god! Justin, whose blood is that?" I ask, my voice shaking as I point towards the kitchen floor. Surely that isn't enough blood for her to be dead somewhere, right? I have no clue. I stand and walk to the kitchen for a closer look.

He scoffs behind me, sounding disgusted. "That little whore thought she could get the best of me," he says, leaning his back against the front door with his arms crossed. I don't know how he looks so calm and collected in this situation, but it's alarming. "Bitch tried to stab me. Can you believe that?" He says and I gasp, my hands coming to my mouth in shock. "Don't be scared, my love, soon she won't be a problem for us anymore," he says, waving his hand through the air as if he's brushing it off.

"Where is she?!" I scream and a sharp slap rings in my ears. I'm stunned momentarily before the pain seeps into my skin. I feel tears stinging my eyes as something warm and wet rolls down my lip. The metallic taste of blood fills my mouth and I know my nose is bleeding from the hit.

"Control yourself, Ember!" He yells at me, "I won't have you acting like such a lunatic. It's embarrassing," he says, coming closer and gripping my chin tightly. I wince at the pain blossoming in my check, but quickly school my emotions. "You'll learn quickly, my dear. I won't tolerate this insolence from you any longer," He says, kissing my cheek where his handprint flames red against my skin.

"I'm sorry," I whisper softly, tears steadily streaming down my face. He releases his grip on my chin and caresses my cheek gently. His touch makes my skin crawl, but I know if I react, he'll only become angrier. "I only worry that if anyone shows up here, you could get in trouble," I say, trying to sound like a concerned lover.

He wraps an arm tightly around my waist, squeezing my hip roughly. "No need to worry, my love," he says, and he pulls me along next to him down the hallway.

We walk towards what used to be my bedroom and I

brace myself for what is waiting for me inside. As we come through the doorway, I can't hold back the loud sob that escapes my lips. In the corner is a dingy mattress and box spring covered in a thin sheet. On top of the sheet, Kelsea lies motionless. I see a gash across her cheek and blood soaks through a spot in her shirt near her hip. I try to watch her chest for movement, any sign that she's still breathing, but I can't tell from this far away.

"This is what will happen to anyone who tries to get between us, Ember. Your friends, your brother, that disgusting ink-covered criminal you allowed to touch you, I will eliminate them all," he says.

I try to close my eyes and will myself to wake up from this nightmare, but a sharp tug on my ponytail tells me this is real. He brings his face closer to mine, pressing his nose against the skin on my neck and inhaling deeply. I move to turn my face away, but he pulls my hair harder, holding me in place. I whimper at the needle-like pain radiating across my scalp and he laughs darkly. He slides his other hand down my body, gripping my breast roughly. I try in vain to escape his hold, but he's too strong.

A knock on the door interrupts his aggressive perusal of my body. He pushes me roughly down to the floor. "You stay here," he says, pulling a gun from his waistband. "You make a sound and I'll put a bullet in that pretty little head of yours, understand?" He asks and I nod quickly. He stalks out of the room towards the front door.

I hear a low, pained moan coming from across the room and turn to see Kelsea's eyes peaking open. I race to her side, holding her still on the mattress. "Hey, it's me, Kelsea, don't worry. Just stay still, okay? I'm gonna get us out of this. God, I'm so sorry this is happening to you," I whisper, brushing her hair back from her face. I have no clue how we're gonna get out of this, but I know this is not where I want my story to end.

thirty-five

Elijah

EVERETT and I pushed our bikes to their fucking limit, but we made it to Durham in record time. We turn off the engines and idle closer to the apartment so the rumble of the pipes doesn't announce our arrival. I spot Ember's Jeep parked in front of the building and my already rushing adrenaline spikes to an all-time high. My woman is in there facing god knows what and I have to get to her.

"What's our plan here, Elijah?" Everett says beside me.

"Just give me a second to think," I say, dialing Breaker's number.

"I've got eyes inside," he says, answering on the first ring. "I can at least see all the elevators and hallways."

"Can you patch it through to my phone?" I ask, my voice sounding hopeful for once today.

"I'm sending you a link now. I'll keep it scanning through each corridor until you tell me where to stop," he says, hanging up as my phone beeps with his incoming message.

I pull up the camera and look through the feed with Everett. "Do you know which unit they're in?" I ask him.

"316. It's right around the corner from the elevator, so we should be able to find some cover if we need it," he says. We both make sure we have one in the chamber before we head inside and up the stairs. With each flight of stairs, my heart beats faster and faster. Adrenaline floods my system and tunnel vision kicks in. All I can see is one step in front of me, my feet carrying me towards Ember. I don't want to think about any other scenario than the one that ends with her in my arms. I'll do whatever it takes to get her and our baby out of here untouched.

We make it to the third floor, and the door to the apartment is right around the corner. More than anything, I want to rush through the door and sweep her out of there. But I know that's more dangerous than making a plan and doing this tactfully. I pull Ev to a stop at the edge of the wall next to the door so we can figure out a way to make this clean.

"We can't go in there guns blazing, Everett," I tell him, seeing the anger barely under control in his eyes.

"Just let me kill this motherfucker, Eli. The world won't miss him," he says, the malice clear in his voice.

"Everett, your sister is pregnant," I make sure he sees the truth in my eyes and understands the magnitude of the situation. He stills, staring directly into my eyes, but his mind is somewhere else. I don't know if it's shock or something else making him react this way, but I don't have time to find out. I didn't want him to find out like this, but I need him to know there's so much more at stake here than just us. He gives me one sharp nod, motioning for me to take the lead. I round the corner and knock on the door, quickly pulling back out of the line of sight if Justin should check the peephole. I just need him to crack the door. Once we're in, I know we can get the upper hand on this son of a bitch.

Every second that passes feels like an eternity. It's like time is moving in slow motion. My skin is crawling with nervous anticipation as I clench and unclench my empty hand. My grip tightens around my pistol as I hear footsteps approaching the door. It cracks open a tiny bit and I see the security chain is still latched. I see Justin's beady eye peering through the crack, and I jump into action. I slam my boot into the center of the door, kicking with all the power I can manage. The chain snaps and I hear a sharp crack as the door connects with his skull. I hear him let out a pained howl, but we don't hesitate. Everett and I both rush through the doorway with our guns drawn. I see him lying on the floor behind the door with blood pouring from his nose, but his hand still has a firm grip on his weapon. Shocking, since I literally knocked him on his ass. He immediately aims it at my chest and fires, but I'm able to dodge in time. I launch my body on top of him, trying to wrestle the gun out of his hand. I hear it clatter to the ground and slide away from us. His legs flail around as he attempts to kick out from under me, but I've got at least a hundred pounds on him. I think I've got him under control, but he places a perfectly timed kick to the side of my knee and I lose my grip on him for just a moment. He scurries quickly to the side of the room to grab the gun as I stumble to my feet.

I hear a scream coming from the bedroom and I don't think. I just run. As I sprint down the hall towards the bedroom, I hear another shot ring out and feel something burn across my neck and cheek, but I don't stop. I hear two more shots and the thump of something hitting the floor and I just pray it isn't Everett. I rush through the doorway to find my girl sitting on her ass against a dirty mattress, her hands covered in blood as she holds a rag against Kelsea's right hip. Black spots dance in front of my vision and I know I've taken a pretty bad hit.

"Ember," is all I can manage before I feel my muscles start to give out. My shoulder slumps against the doorway as the adrenaline wears off and searing pain pushes through. I feel something warm and wet pouring down the side of my face and onto my shoulder, but my arms are too heavy to reach up. I see Ember's beautiful emerald eyes connect with mine and I breathe a sigh of relief. My body feels tingly and sluggish as I slide my back down the nearest wall.

"Elijah!" I hear her scream, her voice sounding shrill and terrified. I can't reach her. I can't move at all. The edges of my vision blur and darken. A hazy figure rushes into the room, coming to my side and holding something against my head. But I can't hold on anymore. I hear someone talking next to me, but I can't understand what they're saying.

Ember's delicate face fills my sight for a second, then everything fades to black.

thirty-six

Ember

6 DAYS. It's been 6 long days since I've seen Elijah's captivating blue eyes. 6 days since I've heard the deep timbre of his voice. 6 days since I've felt the comfort of his arms wrapping around me. Every one of those days I've spent in this incredibly uncomfortable chair next to his hospital bed, listening to the rhythmic beeping of monitors and machines all around us. The doctors have told me every day that he's stable now and he could wake up any time, but I won't believe it until I see those eyes.

I stretch my body over the side of the bed, reaching my arm across his body and placing my hand flat over his heart. I see my engagement ring shine and I think about the happiness I felt the moment I slid it onto my finger. Even if it's only been a week since then, it feels like a lifetime. I slide my free hand over my belly and let a tear fall freely from my eye. What if our baby has to grow up without their father? What if my memories of him are all they ever have? The thought causes a deep ache inside of my chest and I will it away. I won't go there. I need him too badly to even consider that.

It's still crazy to me to think that Justin is dead. It's even crazier to know my brother is the one who killed him. I know I should never be happy about someone losing their life, but I can't find it in myself to feel sad about it. After Justin terrorized me for months, kidnapped my best friend, almost killed her and attempted to kill the man I love, I can't say I'm sorry he's dead. Kelsea lost so much blood in that room I didn't think she would make it through. After everything was said and done, she had to have two blood transfusions and an ovary removed. The doctors told her she may never be able to have children of her own and my heart broke for her. She accepted the information calmly, but I know on the inside she was falling apart. I'm so grateful Everett has been by her side over the past 6 days. I didn't want her to be alone, but I couldn't leave Elijah.

Over the past few days, friends and family have come and gone to check on us both. The second day, I met Elijah and Rory's mother. She is a fantastic woman who obviously loves her children fiercely. She's been incredible, making sure I eat a few things here and there and bringing me fresh clothes every time Rory brings her in. I've made it clear to every person here that I will not leave him. I'd love to see them try to make me. A few other friends of his have come through to check in. It's so obvious he's well loved and respected. A soft knock on the door pulls me from my thoughts and I lift my head to see Rory and her mom coming through the door with coffee cups and breakfast.

"Good morning, dear. How's our boy this mornin'?" Amelia, Elijah's mom, asks with a soft smile. Her southern accent is so thick, I'm shocked Rory and Eli don't sound the same.

"Morning guys," I say, yawning and stretching my arms over my head. "He seems to be doing good. No change, but still good." I accept the large, warm cup of tea she holds out to me.

"Did you sleep at all, honey?" She asks, concern etched all over her face. Even though the circumstances suck, it's nice to feel the care of a mother for once. Even if it's someone else's mother.

"Yeah, here and there." I give her a small smile, hoping she won't see through my lie. Unfortunately, she seems to have the same ability to read me that her son does. My fake smile drops, and she rubs my shoulder reassuringly.

"He's gonna be ok, Ember. My boy is a fighter. He'll find his way back to you, that I know for sure," she says. I look up at her, teary-eyed, and squeeze her hand back. Rory slips out of the room to go find the nurse. She's been a pest to them the entire time we've been here, but I'm grateful for it.

It surprised me to find out that Amelia knew all about Elijah's intentions to propose to me when I met her. Apparently, he's been talking to her regularly about our relationship and she even helped him pick out my ring. It was my turn to surprise her, however, with the news that she was going to be a grandma. She was ecstatic, crying tears of joy and hugging me so tightly I thought we might both pass out. Every day since then, she's been bringing me different teas and snacks that she swears are good for me and the baby and I love her for it. I never imagined I would know what it feels like to be looked after by a mom, but I feel it with Amelia.

"Why don't you take a little break, dear? Take a walk or go visit Kelsea. It's not good for you to sit in this room all day, every day," she says, running her hand over my hair in a nurturing way.

"If he has to be here, then so do I," I tell her, leaving no room for argument. I won't risk the chance that he wakes up and I'm not here. He wouldn't leave me for a second if I was in his place. Amelia walks over and places a kiss on Elijah's forehead, smoothing his long hair back out of his face and smiling down at him. She looks at my rough, tattooed, giant of a man as if he's just a little boy. But I realize that to her he is. He always will be. Instinctively, my hands fall to my own belly as I imagine what having our own little boy or girl will be like. I hope I can be as fierce and loving of a mother as Amelia is. God knows I had plenty of examples growing up of what not to do.

Rory comes through the doorway talking and smiling with a handsome doctor, and Amelia and I both give her a knowing stare. She quickly schools her expression and we nudge each other, snickering under our breath.

"Guys, this is Ezra," she says, still looking at him like a schoolgirl. Amelia clears her throat and Rory snaps out of her daydreams. "Doctor Thompson is Eli's neurologist," she says, and my mind focuses sharply on the man.

"Nice to meet you, Dr. Thompson. Is there anything new you can tell us?" I ask him, not wasting any time.

"Well Mrs. Harding," butterflies flutter in my stomach at the sound of someone calling me that, but I don't bother correcting him. "Your husband's condition is pretty cut and dry. He had massive blood loss from the bullet nicking the artery in his neck. The transfusions we gave him when you all arrived seem to have corrected and stabilized that problem. He sustained some mild trauma to the skull from the bullet's graze, but he should make a full recovery. At this point, his body is just healing itself. We have him on antibiotics to prevent infection and he may need some physical therapy to strengthen the muscles in his neck after he's released." I feel a weight lift from my chest and I take a deep breath.

I'm so relieved to know he's out of the woods. Now if he would just wake up.

"Is there some reason why he's not awake, doctor?" Amelia asks.

"Not any reason in particular, no. He didn't sustain any brain trauma that we are aware of. We will run more extensive tests to be sure once he does wake up. Sometimes the body just uses rest as a defense mechanism. He's had to heal from some pretty significant injuries. It's not uncommon for patients to remain unconscious for several days," he replies. That does nothing to easy my worry.

thirty-seven

Ember

THE NEXT MORNING, I wake with a sense of fear and panic flooding my system. I pull myself from the nightmares that have plagued my sleep recently and I see all is as it has been around me. The monitors beep rhythmically, bringing me comfort. At least I know Elijah is still okay.

Each nightmare ends the same. The paramedics don't get there in time. I'm holding Elijah's lifeless body in my arms and I always wake up with an ache in my chest that feels like I died right next to him. I stand and stretch, rolling my neck and trying to get some circulation back into my aching limbs. If this goes on much longer, I'm going to have to ask for an extra bed or something because this chair just isn't cutting it. I go through my morning routine of brushing my teeth and hair, then walk over to Elijah's bedside to kiss his forehead. As I press my lips to his skin, I hear a small moan escape his lips and I gasp. That's the first noise I've heard from him in a week.

"Elijah? Honey?" I whisper softly, trying not to startle him. I reach out to hold his hand in mine and he gives mine a small squeeze. Happy tears roll down my face before I realize it. That tiny gesture brings me so much joy I can't even breathe. "I'm here, Eli. I'm here." I tell him, squeezing his hand back hard. I push the button to call the nurse into the room.

"Sunshine?" His voice is coarse and breathy. It's barely loud enough for me to hear, but I do. It's the best thing I've ever heard. My head falls onto the side of his arm as my laughter and tears mix together, knowing he's finally made it back to me.

"Yeah, baby, I'm here," I whisper.

"You're okay?" he asks.

"Yeah, I'm okay. Everybody's okay," I say.

"The baby?" his eyes still closed and his expression pained.

"The baby is just fine. We're both okay," I say, laying my hand against his cheek, bring my face down to his. Finally, his eyes flutter open and I see that crystal blue oasis I've been dying to fall into for days. I kiss him softly, careful not to touch his neck.

"Well, you sure know how to make things all about you, don't you, asshole?" I hear my brother's voice coming from the doorway and I look up to see him standing there with Kelsea in a wheelchair in front of him. Elijah chuckles and attempts to sit up, but winces in pain. I grab him by his shoulder and upper arm and help him into a comfortable position with a scowl.

"Don't even start, you two. He just got shot, Everett!" I scold them both and they just smile.

"I'm glad to finally see you showing signs of life, brother," Everett says.

"Yeah, I feel like I got hit by a fucking truck. Or a bullet." Eli says, and I roll my eyes.

"Well, it looks like we're having quite the party in here," the nurse says as she squeezes into the room between Kelsea and Everett. I watch intently as Everett checks her out, but quickly looks away. Kelsea watches him with furrowed brows. I feel like I'm missing something there, but I'm sure I'll get it out of her, eventually.

The next few hours are filled with doctors and nurses coming and going. They poke and prod at Elijah until they're satisfied he's okay. Finally, the doctor tells him we can go home tomorrow as long as all his tests come back in normal range. At some point in the afternoon, Rory and Amelia show up and we all work out a schedule for getting things done once we leave. Even though Elijah insists he'll be fine, I know he won't be able to do a lot for a few weeks, so I'll be glad to have some extra help.

Later that evening, after things have calmed down, I step outside Eli's room while he catches up with my brother. I make it down the narrow hall and barely around the corner before I break. The false smile I've been holding together for days falls and the weight of reality finally sets in. I could have lost him. I could have lost the one man who has shown me how deeply I can love. I push my back against the wall and slide down to the floor until I'm sitting, my arms draped over my knees. Tears flood my eyes as every emotion hits me at once. Fear, anger, desperation, gratitude, love — it's all too much. I sob quietly into my hands, knowing I look like a total basket case to anyone passing by. I'm so grateful to know he's safe now, but knowing how close we came to losing each other is a kind of fear I never want to feel again in my life.

I feel a presence next to me, but I don't lift my head. I can't turn my tears off that easily, so whoever it is will have to deal with it. I feel a warm, comforting arm wrap around my shoulder and immediately recognize the smell of Amelia's perfume. She says nothing, just rubs my shoulder silently, letting me cry until there's nothing left. I reach my hand up to cover hers and we both breathe deeply.

"He's lucky to have found you, my dear," she says quietly.

"I'm the lucky one," I say with a smile. "He's unlike anyone I've ever known. He's so strong and confident, but also kind and generous. I never dreamed I would find a man like him."

"Makes a mama feel good to hear those things. At least I know I did something right raising him," she says, nudging my shoulder. "You'll feel the same one day when your child meets their match. You're perfect for him in every way, Ember. His other half." She speaks so surely. I can see where Elijah learned his confidence.

"You don't know how much it means to me to hear you say that, Amelia," I breathe. "I love him so much it scares me sometimes."

"Thats how you know it's true, honey. It wouldn't be real if it wasn't scary sometimes," she says with a knowing smile. "And you might as well start callin' me mama, sweet girl. Won't be long until it's official anyway, I'm sure." Tears well up in my eyes for a whole new reason this time. Damn. That doctor really wasn't joking about those pregnancy hormones. "Can I ask you something, Em?" she asks me.

"Of course, anything," I reply.

"Your parents..." she trails off as I drop my gaze to the floor. "If it's a sore subject, dear, we don't have to talk about it," she says, patting my hand lightly.

"They're not bad people. They weren't abusive or neglectful. Everett and I never wanted for anything, to be honest." I push my hair back behind my ears and lean my head back against the wall. "They just didn't care for us like parents should. I think when you have children, you should cherish them. You've been given this incredible gift and you should be thankful for that." I place my hand over my belly, rubbing soft circles and smiling. "I already can't wait to see this baby. A parent is supposed to teach their child all these amazing things and I'm so excited. I've always thought my parents had children because they believed that's what was expected of them. They both came from wealthy families, and building a legacy was more important than creating an actual family. By the time Ev and I were in middle school, we were all more like roommates than family. I always promised myself that if I ever had a child, they would never have to wonder if I loved them. This baby will never doubt that," I say with a smile.

She sits silently for a few moments, just absorbing everything I shared with her. "Well, I'm sad for them. They missed out on knowing a truly incredible young woman, Ember. I pray they realize that and make amends before they miss out on a whole new generation," she says, gesturing towards my belly. "But I also hope you know you aren't alone now. My kids may be knuckleheads, but I think I did a decent job of raising them." Her eyes shine with pride as she speaks about her children, and I long for that feeling. "I want you to feel comfortable knowing I'm only a phone call or a short drive away if you need any help. Motherhood is a marathon, my love, not a sprint. So don't expect to master it as soon as this little one arrives. You'll just set yourself up for failure. Motherhood is supposed to be messy and confusing and scary, but also so incredibly rewarding and fulfilling. Watching my children share their happiness with me and succeed in their lives brings me some of the greatest joy I've ever known. You're a strong and capable woman, Ember. You will be an incredible mother. Just remember, we are not who we come from, but who we choose to be." She says, and I realize she's right. I don't have to be like my mother and her mother before her if I don't want to be. I can decide to be whatever kind of mother I want to be.

"And I suppose that brother of yours isn't half bad either," she smirks, and I laugh wholeheartedly at that.

"Yeah, he's okay. I guess I'll keep him around for now," I say, standing and brushing my hands off on my pants. I help Amelia to her feet and we walk back towards Elijah's room together.

thirty-eight

elijah

THE NEXT MORNING, I'm more than ready to get the hell out of this hospital. I'm tired of being poked and prodded like a fucking science experiment, and it's been too long since I've had a decent night's sleep. I tried to coax Ember into the bed with me last night, but she wasn't having it. She was too afraid of hurting me. I won't go another night without her next to me, though.

We load up into the Jeep with Rory and my ma following behind us. Kelsea has to stay in the hospital for a few more days, so Ev said he's staying behind with her. I know there's something going on there, but I'm not gonna push. The only thing I want to think about right now is getting home and decompressing with Ember, getting some kind of normalcy back into our lives.

I give Ember a confused look as we drive right past

the townhouse. "Where are we going, Sunshine?" I ask. She gives me a mischievous grin and points her Jeep towards the edge of town.

"You'll see when we get there," she says with a wide smile. God, I love that smile. I'm the lucky bastard that gets to spend every day waking up next to this woman and I'll do everything I can to be worthy of that honor. Her strength and resilience over the last few months are nothing short of incredible.

"I want to tell you how grateful I am for you, Em," I say, my voice heavy with emotion.

"*You're* grateful for *me*? Shouldn't that be the other way around? Without you, I wouldn't be sitting here today, Elijah," she says, her voice shaking slightly. "I never dreamed I would find someone willing to take a bullet for me... literally,"

Thinking back to that night causes anger to spike through me, but it dissipates quickly, knowing Justin can never touch any of us again. "I'd do it again in a heartbeat, Ember. You and this baby are my life now. Nothing will ever stop me from doing whatever I need to do to take care of you two," I say with conviction.

"I know, honey, and we love you for it," she whispers. Her voice is like a balm for my soul, instantly calming me in a way nothing else ever could.

We turn down a road I know like the back of my hands and I see the plantation come into view. There are several cars parked out front, some I recognize and some

I don't. As we come to a stop, I see nearly a dozen familiar faces file out the front door and it damn near brings me to tears.

"How the hell did you manage this, Ember?" I say, my voice barely above a whisper. These are the men whose lives I've held in my hands, who've held mine in theirs. My entire unit, with the exception of Everett, stands on my front porch, staring back at me now. Tears slide slowly down my face, and I feel no shame as they fall. These men and I have already sacrificed so much for each other. The trials of war have warped and weathered our bodies and minds, but we've always had each other. That is one constant that will never change.

"It's done, Eli," she says, placing her small hand on my wrist. "They all came together to make your dream complete, honey. They were all asking what they could do to help, and Everett suggested this. So they made it happen for you, for us."

I laugh when I see Breaker standing at the end of the line of men. That asshole rarely ever leaves his computer screens for more than an hour, so I'm shocked to see him here. "Damn, even Batman left his cave," I gesture towards him.

"Oh yeah, he was actually the one who coordinated all of this for me," she says, unbuckling her seatbelt and hopping out of the Jeep. She walks around the front end, smiling and waving at the guys as she goes. I'm in awe of this woman, I swear. I open the door and do my best not to wince as I unfold my large frame from the small seat. The pain is manageable, but definitely still there. She takes a step towards the back, but I snag her wrist and pull her into my arms. Out of the corner of my eye, I watch my ma and Rory walk up the steps and hug the guys one at a time.

"I could never repay you for this, Ember. This is amazing," I say, kissing her softly. No one has ever done something so heartfelt and considerate for me.

"Luckily, you'll never have to. This is our home now, Elijah. The home we'll raise our children in. Where we'll celebrate holidays with our families and fight and make up for years and years to come. There's no one I would rather have by my side when the storms come to our doors than you. I feel like every moment in my life has led me here. My choices, my mistakes, my accomplishments, all of it. When I'm with you, my past seems worth it. Because if I'd changed even one thing, I may never have met you." She looks into my eyes with such certainty and devotion that I couldn't doubt her, even if I wanted to. She is my forever. I've known it since I first fell into those stunning green eyes.

epilogue
EMBER

WE'RE all gathered in the main living room. The sound of a dozen large men laughing and joking together is deafening, but at this point, it's music to my ears. After coming so close to losing Eli, I'll spend the rest of my life appreciating the sound of his laughter. I was a little skeptical that the guys could actually pull off the overwhelming amount of work that still had to be done here, but they did. The house looks incredible.

It's so hard to believe that in just a few short months, we'll be bringing our sweet baby into this home. The guys put together a beautiful nursery and I can't wait to show Elijah later tonight. What he doesn't know yet is when he opens those doors, he'll know what he's really in for in about six months. When the paramedics brought us all into the ER after the shooting, the doctors did a very thorough job making sure everything was okay with me considering my condition. With all the extensive tests they ran, they could tell me much more information than the clinic had. I know I must have looked absolutely manic crying and laughing as the doctor explained the results to me, but I just couldn't believe it. Hopefully, Eli will feel the same way I do, though.

As we wave goodbye to the last of our family and friends from the porch, I breathe a sigh of relief. I love them all so much and I'm so grateful for everything they've done for us, but I'm ready to get back into our regular routine. Elijah pulls me tightly into his side and kisses my temple softly. I love it when he does that. It's something that seems so small and simple, but still so intimate.

"I still have one more thing to show you," I tell him.

"Oh, yeah?" He says gruffly, his stubble brushing harshly against the soft skin of my neck as he whispers in my ear. Goosebumps spread across my skin and my heart starts to beat faster, the way it always does when he's close to me this way.

"Nothing like that, Casanova, so get your mind out of the gutter. The doctor hasn't cleared you yet, so there won't be any of that going on here." I step out of his reach and watch his face fall like a little boy.

"Who needs a doctor to clear me? I feel fine. Really, I think I'm good to go," he says with a shrug. I scoff and grab his hand, pulling him into the house behind me.

"Not happening, honey. Besides, I want to show you my new favorite room in the house," I tell him. I try to keep my voice light, but I know I sound excited and nervous all at once. What if this isn't what he wants? What if, after everything we've been through, this is just too much? I know this is just my anxiety getting the better of me, but damn, she's a real bitch.

We make our way through the living room and down the hall towards the master suite. I stop in front of what used to be a small office right next to our bedroom and turn to face Elijah. "You ready?" I ask him with a wide smile.

"Is there a live animal in there or something? I feel like you're building up a lot of suspense for what's behind that door. Did you build a Red Room?" he asks, shooting me a saucy wink and a familiar bolt of pleasure shoots straight to my core at the thought of what we could do with a room like that. I quickly suppress those thoughts and shake the images out of my head.

"Stop it! We had to have a nursery, Elijah," I say, seeing a sudden realization cross his face and his eyes light up with curiosity. "While they were checking me out at the hospital, I found out a few things." I let my words trail off as I back up into the French doors, letting them open wide behind me. I watch as Eli steps through the room, his eyes sweeping over each piece of furniture. The reality hits him as instantaneously as it did me. Two cribs, two rocking chairs, two bouncer seats, two of everything scattered around the room.

"Twins..." he whispers.

"Twins," I reply. I stand in the doorway and let him take a moment to absorb what our future holds. I know from personal experience that twins aren't a walk in the park. Well... maybe Jurassic Park.

"They're sure?" he asks, his back still turned.

"Yes, they're sure. They said one must have been hiding behind the other during our first appointment. Apparently, it's more common than people think," I tell him. I wish he would face me so I could see what he's thinking. Is he as nervous and scared as I am? I walk over to him and place my hand on his shoulder, turning him to face me. I'm shocked to see the tears streaming down his face as he smiles widely.

"You're happy?" I ask, already knowing the answer.

"Of course I am, Sunshine. This is incredible. Do they know if they're boys or girls? Or one of each?" He asks.

"They said they could tell me, but I didn't want to find out without you," I tell him, reaching my hands up and threading them through the long hair at the nape of his neck. He pulls my body flush against his and holds me tightly for several long seconds, just breathing me in.

"I love you, Ember. So fucking much," he says.

"I love you, Elijah. More than I could ever explain." I press my lips to his softly, pouring every ounce of gratitude and love I can manage into this man. I'll spend the rest of my life showing him we can weather any storm that comes between us.

also by sage st. claire

THE GROVEWOOD INK SERIES

Follow these deliciously tattooed men in their pursuits to protect the women who capture their souls. True love and passion are never lacking in the South Carolina Low-Country. These intense alphas have met their matches in the fiery, headstrong women who win their hearts. Stroll down the streets of Grovewood, South Carolina and fall in love with the sprawling Oak Trees dripping in Spanish moss. Love, loss, pain, and pleasure all come together in this sleepy little town.

The Storms Between Us

A brother's best friend romance.

Stay With Me

A friends to lovers romance.

Coming Spring 2023

Tell Me No

An age-gap romance.

Coming Fall 2023

acknowledgments

A huge thank you to my family for always supporting my book addiction and keeping me surrounded by amazing literature. Mama, I know I ruined my eyesight staying up all hours reading in the dark, but nevertheless you persisted. I love you more than words could ever express. This couldn't have happened without your inspiration and carelessness in leaving your Harlequin Romance Novels within my reach!

To my JBH group family, thank you for always answering my endless questions and offering me honest opinions and plenty of girl-power encouragement. The friendship I've found with you guys will nourish my soul for a lifetime. I love you! (except Alison. Fuck you, Alison!)

And to my incredible, amazing, sometimes-stress-inducing husband, you are the reason I believe in fairy tales and love stories. You keep my heart full on days when I feel like my tank is on E. I could never thank the fates enough for bringing you into my life. No measure of time with you could be long enough, but let's start with forever.

about the author

Writing has always been a hobby for Sage St. Claire. However, it was not always something she thought she could make a living with. After deciding it was time to make the leap before turning 30, she realized she had something valuable to share with the world and turned to writing novels.

Since turning her passion into a profession, Sage St. Claire has written prolifically and is constantly exploring new themes, genres and ideas. It's incredibly hard work, but she's never happier than when she sit's down at her desk with a LARGE cup of coffee to put the opening words to a new novel on paper.

www.sagestclaire.com

facebook.com/SageStClaireAuthor
instagram.com/sagestclairebooks
goodreads.com/sagestclaire
tiktok.com/@sagestclairebooks

Ember Blake isn't looking for love.
After graduating college and escaping her abusive ex, she's only interested in moving on with her life. But the shadows of her past send her running as fast as she can to the safety of her twin brother... and his dangerously handsome best friend.

Elijah Harding is content to live his life one tattoo at a time.
At 29, he's worked hard to create a legitimate name for himself by opening a tattoo shop of his own. But when his best friend's twin sister comes barreling into his life unexpectedly, he finds himself drawn to her despite his best efforts to stay away.

Ember would give anything to be free of the darkness following her. Elijah will stop at nothing to keep her out of harm's way. Will their love be strong enough to weather the storms between them?

WWW.SAGESTCLAIRE.COM

ISBN 979-8-218-05527-1